THE RED RIGHT HAND

JOEL TOWNSLEY ROGERS

Introduction by
JOE R. LANSDALE

AMERICAN MYSTERY CLASSICS

Penzler Publishers
New York

Published in 2020 by Penzler Publishers
58 Warren Street, New York, NY 10007
penzlerpublishers.com

Distributed by W. W. Norton

Cover image: Andy Ross
Cover design: Mauricio Diaz

Paperback ISBN 978-1-61316-165-4
Hardcover ISBN 978-1-61316-164-7
eBook ISBN 978-1-61316-163-0

Library of Congress Control Number: 2020907350

Printed in the United States of America

9 8 7 6 5 4 3 2 1

INTRODUCTION

READING *The Red Right Hand* is a bit of a hallucinogenic adventure, or at least as close as I've come to that sort of feeling, since the idea of a drug-induced experience has never been of interest to me.

But a book-induced one. I'm all for that. And *The Red Right Hand* is just the pill to take.

Before discussing the novel, I should point out that Joel Townsley Rogers wrote a lot—nearly all of it short stories for the pulp magazines. If these stories are available, collected, I'm unaware of it. But he is responsible for at least four novels, and this one is the one that has managed to avoid the erosion of time.

There is a short interview/article on Rogers in the edition I read, but it only manages to heat up the desire to know more about the author. This much is certain: he seems less impressed with his novel than the rest of us are, and feels that it is only a minor representative of his long career. It was all in a day's work. Still, in a garden of delights there is often one flower that is more exceptional than the others, and this book seems to be Rogers's magnificent orchid.

At times, while reading Rogers's peculiar book, I felt as if I were seeing the world through a dark and grease-smeared window pane that would frequently turn clear and light up in spewing colors like a firework display on the Fourth of July. At the same time there was the sensation of something damp and dark creeping up behind me, a cold chill on the back of my neck.

Clues and odd impressions pile up like plague victims, and from time to time the answer to the riddle seems close at hand, as if you could reach out and grasp it. Then the answer that seemed so clear wriggles from your grasp like an electric eel and slithers into darkness.

The largest part of the novel's appeal for me was the style in which it was written, a near stream-of- consciousness akin to the flip-side of pulp, more like the literary novels of William Faulkner or some of the more experimental novels of one of my personal favorites, Fredric Brown. At moments the novel seemed to preview the coming of writers like Jack Kerouac, who would someday write *On the Road* in a rolling rhythm reminiscent of a car racing down a dark, empty highway with the headlights turned off.

It's a novel that certainly fits, red herring- and clue-wise, within the Golden Age of mystery, but it is far more stylistically adventurous than most of the clue-on-clue novels of that era. And it is at the same time something else: an outlier straddling the fence, one leg on the side of the Golden Age mystery, the other on the side of the psychological and somewhat hardboiled school of storytelling. It has a bit of the Alfred Hitchcock mode of storytelling as well, one damn thing after another. It owes a debt to horror fiction, and perhaps a greater debt to creep-up-on-you writers like John Dickson Carr. But, like any good recipe that borrows from existing ones, it eventually evolves into its own thing and in the end stands apart as something inimitable.

The story moves back and forth in time, akin to the natural thought process, as if the whole thing were spilling out of the narrator's brain from moment to moment, and we were seeing all the in-betweens of thought. Little details about how, when given a cigar, the author makes note of the rarity of him smoking one, states how it's a special occasion. There are a number of these seemingly unimportant asides that gradually help shape a believable, if not necessarily reliable, narrator. It gives the story a feeling of pleasant discomfort, like a bolt-rattling carnival ride with the sound of muted laughter below, and above the sick aura of cheap lights, and above that, the moon, full and cloud-coated.

There really isn't any way to capture *The Red Right Hand* in a net so as to have it pinned and labeled. It's not a butterfly. It's a genre slider, a brain teaser, a liar and a truth-teller all at the same time. There are moments when you sense misdirection, but at the same time you are willing to take that detour because there is something of the primitive back-brain about all of it, guiding us as readers to not let go of the narrator's hand for fear of being lost in the dark.

I'll go no further discussing the workings of this novel for fear of wounding the bird, so to speak. For explaining too much about how the bird flies would take away from its regal mystery and just might break its dark, beautiful wings.

The novel's rolling rhythm of reversals and revelations make this a straight-through read. I suggest you prepare for that. Find a special time to be immersed in the novel. That is the best way to enjoy it, since there are no chapter breaks. It is best if the spell remains unbroken.

If at all possible, choose a night when you are rested and satisfied. It wouldn't hurt if there is a rain storm. Not enough to blow the lights out, but enough to make the wind howl and the rain clatter against the roof. Sit by a window if you can, a single lamp illuminating your reading space. And if there happens to be a roll of thunder that shakes the window panes, a stitch of lightning that strobes your reading space, all the better. A blanket over your knees would be nice. A big cup of hot chocolate at your elbow would help the mood, the steam from it rising out of the cup in a fast-fading cloud.

Deep dive, and keep right on reading until the sun comes up and the book is closed. When that's done, you'll need a few moments to absorb it all, to let the magic soak into your bones and to realize that you have read a singular representative of when a writer's talent, ideas, and state of mind have happily collided to produce a masterpiece.

—JOE R. LANSDALE

THE RED
RIGHT HAND

THERE is one thing that is most important, in all the dark mystery of tonight, and that is how that ugly little auburn-haired red-eyed man, with his torn ear and his sharp dog-pointed teeth, with his twisted corkscrew legs and his truncated height, and all the other extraordinary details about him, could have got away and vanished so completely from the face of the countryside after killing Inis St. Erme.

That is Point One of the whole problem. Point Two is the question of what he did with St. Erme's right hand, if the state troopers and the posse of neighboring farmers haven't yet found it on the Swamp Road, along with the rest of the young millionaire bridegroom's body, by the time I have finished setting down the details for analysis. For St. Erme had a right hand, that much is indisputable. And it must be found.

Those are the two most essential questions in the sinister problem that confronts me—the problem I must examine carefully in every detail, and find an answer to without a needless moment of delay. Before that killer strikes me down as he struck old MacComerou, the famous murder psychologist, with his keen old brain, who had got too close to him in some way, it seems. And how many others out in the darkness where they are hunting him, there is no saying yet.

To be answered, therefore:

1. How does he manage to remain unseen?

2. Assuming that his brain is not just a dead jumble of loose cogwheels and broken springs, what is he trying to accomplish—what makes him tick?

With an answer to those two questions, or either one of them, the police feel that they would have him stopped.

And yet those aren't the only questions, the only baffling aspects of the problem. No less inexplicable—to me, at least—is the puzzle, from the beginning, of how that smoke-gray murder car, with its blood-red upholstery and high-pitched wailing horn, could have passed by me while I was at the entrance to the Swamp Road just before twilight, with St. Erme in it dying or dead already, and that grinning little hobo murderer driving it like a fiend.

Was I, Harry Riddle, Dr. Henry N. Riddle, Jr., of St. John's Medical and New York S. & P.—alert and observant, pragmatic and self-contained surgeon as I like to think myself—asleep with my eyes open? Could it have been a temporary total blanking out of consciousness—a kind of cataleptic trance, descending on me without warning and leaving no trace or realization of its occurrence afterward—which made me fail to see, or at all to be aware of, that death car rushing up the narrow stony road to the fork while I was trying to get my own stalled car started there, and veering off onto the Swamp Road beside me, so close that its door latches must have almost scraped me, and the pebbles shot out by its streaking tires have flicked against my ankles, and the killer's grinning face behind the wheel been within an arm's length of my own as he shot by?

Or was there something darker than a mental lacuna and a moment of sleepwalking on my part? Was there something vaporous and phantasmagorical, was there something supernatural and invisible—was there, in short, something hellish and *impossible* about that rushing car, about its red-eyed sawed-off little driver and its dead passenger, which caused me to miss it complete?

For certainly I missed it. I did not see it. I have stated that to Lieutenant Rosenblatt and his troopers in unequivocal words, over and over; and I will not be budged from the assertion. And I think that old MacComerou was beginning at last to believe me a little, and to see some significance in the item; though I am afraid the police still do not.

It is possible, of course, that I place an undue amount of emphasis on the matter in my own mind. Still, it continues to bother me—my failure to see that murder car—because it involves the validity of my own sense perceptions and mental operations, which I have never felt it necessary to certify to myself before.

The question is set down, I find, in Lieutenant Rosenblatt's fat cardboard-covered notebook, in which he painstakingly recorded all his inquiries earlier in the night, and which he left behind him on the table in MacComerou's living room here when he last went out.

> Q. [To Dr. Riddle] And you were at the Swamp Road entrance all during the murder hour, Dr. Riddle?
> A. I was.
> Q. And you did not see the car pass by at all?
> A. I did not see it.
> Q. You have heard the detailed description of the killer, Doctor, as given by Miss Darrie here, Mr. St. Erme's fiancée, and by others who saw him. But you did not see him yourself?
> A. I did not see him. To the best of my knowledge, I have never seen him.
> Q. You'll stand on that?
> A. I'll stand on that. . . .

And so I must.

In the larger view, of course, it makes no actual difference whether or not I saw the murder car go by, since obviously it did go by. Other men saw it all the way along the road, all the way from Dead Bridegroom's Pond to just before it reached me, and to them it was not invisible or a phantom. It struck big shambling John Flail as he was walking homeward just around the bend from me, and to him—for one dreadful moment, as he tried to spring out of its way with a bleating cry, hearing that demon at the wheel laughing, and feeling the iron blow smash the bones within his flesh like glass—it could certainly have been no phantom. Old Mac-Comerou himself saw it pass his place while he was digging in his garden, with sufficient detail to recognize St. Erme as the stricken man in it, if not the extraordinary little demon at the wheel. And Elinor Darrie, moreover, previously in the day, had driven it a hundred miles up from New York City, on her wedding trip with her handsome, black-eyed lover, who was soon to die.

They have found it now, finally, down on the Swamp Road where the killer abandoned it after he had passed me by, with its engine still warm and its cushions blood-soaked—a gray Cadillac eight-cylinder sport touring, last of production '42, made of steel and aluminum, leather, rubber, glass, and all the other ordinary, solid, visible materials, with its engine and chassis numbers that were stamped on it in the factory, and its Federal tax and gas stickers on its windshield, and its license plate XL 465-297 NY '45, together with the coupon books and registration of its owner in its glove compartment, A. M. Dexter of Dexter's Day and Nite Garage, 619 West 14th Street, New York City, who has confirmed by long distance that he lent it to St. Erme. A beautifully kept car, with less than five thousand miles on its speedometer, worth at least thirty-five hundred dollars by OPA prices anywhere today, and certainly no phantom.

They have found poor Inis St. Erme's body, too, so he was not a phantom, either. Only the little man with the red eyes and the torn car—the man in the blue saw-tooth hat, the man who had no name—they haven't yet quite found.

And so that aspect of the problem—the puzzle of the murder car's singular and specific invisibility to me, and to me alone—must be set aside, for the time being, anyway. Whether to be answered finally or never answered makes no difference now.

The thing that I have to consider now without delay—the thing that I have to consider most intensely, and with all my mind, and *now* (now, sitting here at the desk in Mac-Comerou's dusty, old-fashioned country living room, with St. Erme's young bride asleep on the old horsehair sofa beside me, and the hot moonless night still black out-of-doors, though the dawn must break eventually—now, with the lanterns and flashlights moving out in the darkness, and the voices of the troopers and posse men near and far off, calling to each other with the thin, empty sound which men's voices have in the night; and some of them dropping back a while ago to get hot coffee from the pot left brewing on the kitchen range, with their grim tired faces swollen from mosquito bites and their legs covered to the knees with swamp muck and damp sawdust from the old sawmill pits, glancing in at me and the sleeping girl through the kitchen doorway only briefly while they gulped their drink in deep draughts to keep their brains awake, shaking their heads, in answer to my silent question, to indicate they had found no trace yet, and then out again on farther trails, with an empty slam of the screen door behind them—and now with the lanterns moving farther off through the woods and swamps, over the hills and down into the hollows; and now the distant baying of the hounds that have been brought in from somewhere; and armed men in pairs and squads patrolling every road for miles around, ready to shoot down at the rustle of a leaf that crazy little killer, with his bloody saw-tooth knife and fanged grin, creeping so cunningly and red-handed through the dark)—the thing that I have to consider here and without delay, in this deep darkness near the end of night, is this thing, and this thing only:

Where is that killer now?

For I have a cold and dismal feeling that he is somewhere near me, no matter how far off the lanterns move and the voices call and the far hounds bay. And near the sleeping girl beside me, his victim's young wife to be. A feeling that he will strike again. That he knows I am somehow dangerous to him. Though how, I cannot yet perceive.

Somewhere in the darkness outside the window. Watching me from the black garden.

Or nearer even than that, perhaps. Inside this creaky two-hundred-year-old-hill-country farmhouse itself, it may be, so silent now and temporarily deserted of the hunters.

A feeling of his silent sardonic laughter because I cannot see him.

Of the murder in his watching eyes.

There was a scuttling across the attic floor overhead a few moments ago, but it was probably only a squirrel or a rat.

There seem to be a number of them which have been allowed to make their nests in the old house.

There was the creak of a floorboard just now beyond the door of the small back pantry or woodshed off the kitchen where old MacComerou kept his garden tools. But when I held my pencil and listened for the sound again, turning my eyes, it was not repeated. Old boards sometimes creak that way in old houses. With no step upon them.

The old-fashioned golden-oak wall telephone beside the stove out in the kitchen gives a brief jangle every now and then, but it is not ringing the house here.

It is a party line, and the ring here is five long, five short. It is not ringing any number. Just the jangle of free electricity in the bell.

I must not permit such slight and meaningless sounds to distract me from the problem. Still there is a perfectly human urge I feel to listen every instant, and to turn my eyes to the shadows around me, while I make my notes.

I am not a professional policeman, nor what is known as an amateur detective. Crime does not fascinate me. It is no part of my instinct to be a man-hunter, but to save life.

Yet, as a surgeon I am, I trust, reasonably well disciplined in the scientific method, with a basic instinct for looking at facts objectively. I am analytical and observant, and have always made a habit of noting little details of all sorts to tuck away in the pigeonholes of my mind.

And out of all those details which I have casually noted

and idly tucked away during the past few hours, it is possible that I may be able to arrive at some rational and unsupernatural explanation of where the killer is. And of what he is—a man, and neither a hallucination nor a demon. Provided only that I bring all these details forth to the last one, omitting none of them, however trivial they are or seem to be.

It is the thing which I must do now, to the exclusion of all else. There is a killer loose. There is a malignancy to be located and excised. It is a problem in diagnosis, nothing more.

I must set the facts down for examination, in the method of a case history preliminary to a surgical diagnosis. It is a tedious process, but it is the only conclusive way. A thousand bright formless intuitions may go rushing through a man's mind as quick as lightning, if he will let them; and each may seem to flash with blinding brilliance for an instant. Yet they leave no definite shape behind them when they have faded out, and there is only the dark again, a little deeper than it was before. Facts which are set down on paper, however, have substance, and they have a shape. They can be measured and compared. They can all be added up.

That is the method in which I have always found it necessary to do my own thinking, anyway. And I must discipline myself to use that method now. If there is time.

Let the others continue to hunt him through the darkness. Let them find more bodies of his dead. They have done that, too, I seem to have heard them shouting back and forth, far off a little while ago. With the hounds howling. But they haven't found *him* yet. And why not?

There is some item missing from the puzzle, or there is some item too many. I must assemble all the pieces, and work it out. To find the answer to that dead man I saw walking. And of where Corkscrew is now—the ragged man, the little sawed-off man, the grinning dirty man with the matted auburn hair who had a voice so strangely like my own.

For that is something which I must answer, too. It is an item never to forget.

Perhaps, if I could only see it, the answer to him lies before my eyes.

Very well. I am here. I will start here.

I am sitting at the battered secretary-desk in the living room of the summer home of the late Adam MacComerou, professor emeritus of psychiatry at Harvard. It is situated on the Whippleville-Stony Falls Road, in the northern Connecticut hills, a hundred miles from New York. The hour is half-past three of the morning, of Thursday, August 11.

There is a quire of yellow work paper and a sheaf of sharpened pencils on the desk blotter pad. The green-shaded gasoline study lamp gives a white steady light for writing.

In the glass doors of the secretary I can see my reflection when I glance up, and the room behind me to the farthest limits of the light. That man with the round head covered with close-clipped reddish hair, with the red-brown eyes and the brown thickly freckled face, is myself, Harry Riddle, Dr. Henry N. Riddle, Jr. That's me, myself. The self that I have always known, for twenty-seven years.

The bookshelves back of the glass doors are filled with a varied assortment of old MacComerou's ponderous reference books. There is a bright red *Who's Who in America*. A bright green *Garden Flowers, Their Planting and Cultivation*. In between them stands a somber brown buckram-bound copy, six inches thick, of the old man's own monumental *Homicidal Psychopathology*, his tremendous textbook analysis of the murderous mind, which has been a classic in every medical school's advanced psychology course for more than a generation, and has gone through how many editions I don't know.

In the desk's pigeonholes there are sheaves of papers—brief clinical notes and case-history jottings, apparently, I find on pulling one or two of them forth, for some sequel which he may have intended writing to that great tome, set down in a small, spidery, old-fashioned hand.

The case of A, of good family, well educated, colossally conceited of own mental powers, who at age 45, unsuccessful in all his undertakings and greedy for money, plots uncle's death so as to inherit modest fortune——

So one paper reads. But whether A succeeded in his murderous plans or not before he was discovered is not told, nor what retribution he met with. It is a story not completed, for a book that will never be written. Which lies now, with much else about murder, in a dead man's mind.

Besides the quire of work paper on the desk, there is a

small memo pad which had three or four notations on it, in the same wavering but careful hand:

Call Barnaby & Barnaby GU 9-6400 after lunch
Inquire about mail
Have John Flail clear out cesspool & prune privet, after painting house & barn
Sugar, matches, potatoes, oranges, bacon, strawberries, bread

Commonplace notes about the little business of daily living which a man must plan for, living alone in the country. Little things to be done to keep the place up. Provisions to be got. A phone call to his lawyers or publishers, perhaps. No murder there.

A folded newspaper, for a third item, lies beside the lamp on the desk—a copy of the Danbury *Evening Star,* dated Wednesday, August 10, yesterday afternoon, with big headlines on it about some great amphibious operation against Japan itself, it seems.

HONSHU INVADED!

There are radioed photographs and lesser headlines over the whole portion of page that is visible. Perhaps the fate of the world for generations is being decided in that terrific battle which is told about. Hundreds of thousands of our men, at this very moment, must be locked in a fury of desperate struggle. The story of it is here. Yet such is our concentration on our own immediate affairs, on our own small lives and the terror of our deaths, that no one has opened the news-paper to read it since it came. No one has had time. Nor will anyone read it now, since the news in it, in these last few hours, has grown already stale.

In addition, I have on the desk Lieutenant Rosenblatt's fat pulp-paper notebook, which he left behind when he went surging out, with his wrinkled pugdog face, with his stocky little frame in his blue black-belted uniform, reaching for his gun, at Quelch's scream from near John Flail's.

More than an hour ago, and Rosenblatt has not been back since. So I have appropriated his notebook, to examine it for anything which I may have overlooked.

Those are the only things I see in front of me, as I sit here. I do not see how the killer could be hidden in books on the secretary shelves, or in papers on the desk, or in my reflection in the glass. If there is any trace or pattern of him visible, I do not see it.

Perhaps old Adam MacComerou saw some pattern, with his big old brain that knew so much of murder. But if he did, he could not help himself. No one near him when he met the killer. He left no word that has been found.

Yet now, sitting here at the desk where he had his larg-est thoughts, I feel nearer to him than when I was walking down the road with him in the twilight, looking for that spectral gray car which had vanished, neither of us knowing yet that it was murder, though with something dreadful in the air, hearing the croaking in the weeds beside the road.

No, the croaking had stopped then. Still I felt him alien and remote from me, though he was beside me, then. But now and here, I have almost a feeling that he is trying to help me. That he would help me if he could.

At my left there is the doorway going out into the kitchen, where the wood range gives forth a low dull heat and the phone bell jangles and the alarm clock ticks. There is a lamp on the shelf above the sink out there, and I can see the whole room fairly clearly, to the whitewashed planks of the woodshed door beyond, with its H hinges and rusty latch.

Back of my left shoulder, here in the living room, there is the closed door into the bedroom. Behind me, at the farther end of the room, is the door into the small front hallway, with the stairway out in it leading up to the half-story attic. But the front door is padlocked and nailed, and the door into the hallway itself is locked with a key.

Through the open window at my right hand the mingled odor of yellow roses and damp night grass and rich black garden earth comes in. Moths are fluttering against the copper window screen, with soft repeated bumpings of their white dusty bodies, their crimson eyes reflecting in the light.

On the sofa against the wall, beside the desk, St. Erme's young bride is still sleeping deeply. She fell off that way about one o'clock, Rosenblatt told me when I returned, while he was going over his notes. Worn out by nervous strain, by sheer physical exhaustion and all the black nameless terror, yet able to dream it all away now for a little while, one hopes, with the unequaled recuperative powers of nineteen.

She has not been told yet that St. Erme's body has been found. I, or someone else, will have the obligation of telling her when she awakes. But perhaps it will not be necessary for her ever to be told anything more.

The tautness has slipped away from her. She is completely relaxed. Her slight body, in her periwinkle-blue gown and thin white summer coat with the little rabbit's fur at the collar, is lying with knees bent sideward, with her face turned away from me and the light. Her breathing is faint and almost cataleptic, without a visible stirring of her breast. Her dark blue eyes, with their enormous pupils, which were so full of terror at first sight of me, are closed now beneath a sweep of lashes. Her left arm has dropped down off the sofa's edge, with knuckles trailing to the floor. The big emerald engagement ring given her by St. Erme, too large for her finger, lies on the roses of the carpet in the shadows, in danger of slipping off. Yet it might disturb her if I tried to remove it for safekeeping.

She has turned her head just now on the sofa's headrest, and her face is toward me. A faint sweat is on her forehead and short upper lip, from the still heat of the night. A strand of dark curl is plastered to her temples. Her lips are a little parted, breathing more deeply now.

The edge of the lamplight falls on her breast and the lower part of her face. But by propping up the newspaper in a kind of screen, I have succeeded in shielding it from her eyelids partially. So there is a shadow on her look. But none, I hope, in her dreams. Until she wakes.

The voices of the men out in the night have gone beyond earshot now. The rats and squirrels in the attic have ceased their scuttering. There is no board in all the house that creaks. The fragile beating of the insects at the screen will not disturb her. My pencil moving on the page.

So I must examine the problem in every detail, setting the facts down.

First, there is she herself. What do I know about her, since she is here?

It was just after dark when I first met her, stumbling along the stony road from the lake shore eight miles below, bewildered, terrified, and lost.

I had been trying to make up time in my old car, after the lost hour while I had been stalled at the Swamp Road entrance, and was expecting to strike the main highway soon, to get back down to New York.

But it was still a nightmare road, narrow and stony, winding between steep wooded slopes and big rocks which pressed out on the road shoulders on either side, as it had been since I first got on it. No other cars, and not half a dozen inhabited places that I had passed.

Rounding a sharp rock turn, I saw her white figure, pressed back at the right side of the road, in my headlights.

Like an unearthly shape in some Coleridgian poem, gesturing imploringly to me.

Her eyes were enormous and dark in her pale face. There were scratches and dirt streaks on her cheeks, and dead leaves in her dark hair. Clusters of green and brown burrs were caught on her coat. Her white pumps were muddy and stone-bruised, and one of them had lost its heel.

She had nothing in her hands, not even a pocketbook—she had left her purse in the car, along with everything else, when she and St. Erme had got out. It would still be in the car when it would be found down on the Swamp Road, though emptied of the fifty-dollar bill St. Erme had given her at the bank before they started, and even of its small change.

She was breathing hard from her scrambling and running, trembling, as I stopped beside her.

"Please!" she gasped. "Can you give me a lift somewhere? He kidnaped my fiancé and stole our car! He was trying to find me! There is no one who seems to live around here at all! I thought no one was ever going to come by!"

"Get in," I said, opening the door on her side. "We'll get you to the police."

She recoiled against the rock wall.

"Get in," I repeated to her soothingly. "We'll try to find him. Who was he?"

"O dear God!" she gasped. "Doc!"

She must have thought I was going to reach out and grab her, in that moment. Turning with that frantic gasp, she started to run toward the front of the car, down the road ahead.

"Wait a minute!" I said. "Confound it, what's the matter with you?"

There is only one way to deal with hysteria, and that's to jump on it. Whatever had caused her frantic terror, she had to be stopped before she had hurt herself. I opened the car door, and was out after her in a leap.

She was too exhausted to run far. She tripped on her pump heel in no more than half a dozen steps, and, with a sob, fell on hands and knees on the road.

"Stand up!" I said, getting her under the armpits. "You aren't hurt, are you?"

I lifted her to her feet and turned her around to face me, with my hands still on her arms. Her face was bloodless in the headlights, and she stood limp and almost cold within my grasp.

"Snap out of it!" I said. "Nothing has got you. I'm not the bogey man. You're all right."

She stared at me with dilated pupils, as I slowly released her. Her gaze seemed to go over each feature of my face twice.

"Why, you aren't!" she said. "Are you?"

A deep shudder passed through her, and her frozen look relaxed.

"Of course not," she said. "I'm sorry. He was much smaller and older, and his hair was matted, and he needed a shave. And he was dressed so extraordinarily. But I am a little nearsighted. And when you spoke to me, your voice——"

A little nearsighted. She was probably damned myopic.

"I am Dr. Riddle," I said. "Dr. Harry Riddle of New York. You say your car has been stolen and your fiancé kidnaped? Was it a gray Cadillac phaeton with red upholstery, and a license plate XL something?"

"Yes!" she said. "That was it! You noticed it as it went past you?"

"Was your fiancé named Inis St. Erme?" I said. "A black-eyed man, rather tall, with black hair and a black mustache, in a gray gabardine suit and a Panama hat?"

"Yes!" she told me, still a little incoherent. "Do you know Inis? I am Elinor Darrie. We were on our way to Vermont to be married. How did you know who I was? We picked up this hitchhiker outside of Danbury, the most horrible-looking little man you could imagine——"

"A little tramp with red eyes and long matted auburn hair?" I said. "With sharp pointed teeth and a torn left ear, about five feet three inches high? Dressed in a checked black and white sport coat, a green shirt, and a light blue felt hat with the brim cut away in scallops all around?"

"That was the man?" she said. "Do you know him? What did he do to Inis? Please tell me! Where is Inis now?"

"I don't know," I said. "I haven't seen him."

"He wasn't in the car any longer when it passed you? That must mean——"

"I didn't see your car," I told her.

"You didn't see it?"

"No," I said. "I didn't see it. I didn't see your fiancé, I'm sorry. I didn't see the tramp, either. But he drove up the road, apparently, and he had your fiancé with him. Get in, and I'll turn around. There's a phone at a house a few miles back up the road, if no place nearer. The police have already been notified, I think. He killed a man—ran him down. No, not your fiancé. Just a man walking on the road. Don't worry. Everything is probably all right. He can't have got far. Your fiancé will probably be found."

I got her into my coupe, and started on down the road with her, looking for a place to turn around. My assurances, though mere empty banalities, had succeeded somewhat in assuaging her. Being in a car and going somewhere, too. No longer alone on the dark empty road.

"I hope I shan't be taking you out of your way," she said with childish apology. "I suppose maybe I was an awful fool to let myself be so frightened. But he did do something to Inis, and he did drive off with him. Are you sure that you don't have to go some place in a hurry—that you can spare the time?"

"That's all right," I said. "I was just on my way down from Vermont."

"We were going to Vermont ourselves," she said. "We were going up there to be married. We couldn't get married in Danbury today, we found, and so we thought we would drive on up. Then just outside of Danbury we met this tramp——"

"You'll find a bottle of alcohol and some cleansing tissues in the glove compartment in front of you," I told her. "There's a comb, too, I think. It will make you feel better to freshen up. I'll turn the mirror around for you. Has that got it? Try not to think of him any more now for the moment. Think of yourself or think of me. It will probably turn out all right. Let's leave it for the police."

I switched on the dome light above. Obediently she wetted a tissue and cleaned her face, then scrubbed her hands, with the gravity of a kitten. She found the comb and combed her dark hair, which is one of the most pleasurable and self-soothing gestures which a woman can make, as well as one of the most agreeable to be in proximity to while it is being made.

"You are very kind," she said, with her lower lip still trembling a little. "Did you say your name was Riddle? Why, I work for a man named Riddle. Mr. Paul Riddle of the Riddle Insurance Agency on East Forty-fourth. You are from New York, too, you said? Are you a doctor, really?"

"That's right," I told her. "Dr. Harry Riddle. On the staff of St. John's Medical and Surgeons' and Physicians'. I live at 511 West Eleventh Street. I belong to the University Club, the Scalpel, and the Dutch Treat. I am a Republican, and white. My father had a second cousin named Paul Riddle who is an insurance man, I think. I don't know him, but he's the same family. If that helps to make it right."

"511 West Eleventh?" she said. "Do you live there, actually? Why, that's the big apartment house right across from me. I live at 514, one of the old brownstones opposite, if you've ever noticed. Isn't that extraordinary? I've been living there four months. It seems as if I should almost know you. But I've never seen you before, have I?"

"Not that I know of," I told her. "I've never seen you, anyway. But New York's like that. We're neighbors across the street, and we've got to get a hundred miles away from it, on a lonely road, to meet."

"Do you happen to know who the man is who lives in the second-floor apartment at the end, in your building?" she asked me naïvely.

"Why?" I said. "Has someone there been training field glasses on you?"

"Why, yes," she said, somewhat embarrassed. "How did you know? I hadn't realized he had been doing it. But one time when Inis was waiting to take me out to dinner, he noticed someone behind the curtains in the window across, watching with glasses. I always pulled my shades down after that."

"When a man wants to know who lives in the apartment opposite, it's always a pretty girl," I said. "When a pretty girl wants to know, it's generally a man with field glasses. One of the most popular of New York sports. I don't know who lives on the second floor. I live on the fourteenth in the rear, myself, I'm sorry."

"Oh, I didn't mean that I thought that you——" she said.

"I was just thinking of the apartment house you live in, that looms so big across from me, so many hundreds of people living in it. Naturally it wouldn't have been you."

"Why not?" I said. "You're pretty, and I look human, I hope. If I lived on the second floor, and had field glasses. Still, a doctor gets to see a good deal of anatomy in the course of his trade. We're neighbors, anyway, that's been established, and I'm probably related to your boss. What are you, a secretary?"

"A receptionist," she told me. "That is, I was. I quit yesterday to get married. We were going to get married in Danbury, but they have a five-day law. Then we started up for Vermont, and met this man——"

She put the comb away. Her lip had stopped trembling. She looked, and no doubt felt, more controlled now.

"You're all right," I said. "Tell me about it now, as well as you can. What happened?"

It was a simple enough incident, in its general aspects. She and St. Erme had picked up the tramp a little before sunset, outside of Danbury, fifty or sixty miles below. A repellent-looking little man, but St. Erme had felt sorry for him. They had turned off from the main road onto this side road to have a picnic supper by a lake, a little distance down from where I had met her.

They had left the tramp in the car with their baggage and provisions, while they had gone down through woods to the lake shore to look the site over, to see if it was suitable. She and St. Erme had reached the lake, and St. Erme beside her was just bending to gather some stones to build a rude fireplace, when she had glanced up and seen the tramp peering over a mossy rock ledge directly above them.

He had sneaked down after them, a quarter mile from the car, perhaps only to spy on them out of curiosity, it might seem. But she had already been a little disturbed by him, and at the apparition of him peering there above her, with his ugly little red eyes beneath his saw-tooth hat, in the silence and the silver twilight, by the black waters of the deep quiet lake, she had been completely terrified. She had screamed with all her voice.

"Don't!" she had screamed.

Not with any clear idea that he intended to do anything to St. Erme or her, but wanting him to go away.

St. Erme had been straightening up, with a rock in his hand, at her cry. He had seen the tramp spying above and had been enraged. With an oath he had let the rock fly at the fellow, who had dodged and fled. Crashing through the underbrush, he had fled back up toward the road where the car was parked.

St. Erme had pursued him furiously, thinking perhaps to give him a shaking or a thrashing for the fright he had caused her. A big man, with a powerful physique, he must have despised the little sneaking fellow. No thought of danger to himself. Of that knife back in the car.

Scrambling frantically up the wooded hillslope after, she had heard a hoarse inhuman scream from the road above, followed by a giggling skin-crawling sound like laughter, and then a silence.

She had been terrified. Abandoning her white coat, too easily seen, she had hidden in the bushes. Presently the tramp had come stalking her. She had caught a glimpse of him in his checked jacket and scalloped hat, with something in his right hand. His eyes, which had been small and red, now looked extraordinarily pale, the pale of ice and freezing murder.

Crouching and skulking, he had passed her within thirty feet, going down toward the lake shore where he perhaps expected to find her still, and then coming swiftly back up again, before she could get up to the car, calling her name and swearing, with a low snarling voice like a maniac or an animal, while she hid in a paralyzed bird terror.

He had found her coat where she had left it, picking it up and shaking it, and hurling it down again. For a long time—for hours, it had seemed to her, though it might not have been more than ten or twenty minutes—she had silently crept and hidden from him in desperate silent fright in the darkening twilight woods, with him never more than a hundred or two feet away.

He had given up trying to find her eventually, and had gone back to the car. She had worked up near enough to the road by then to see St. Erme sprawled motionless in the front seat, with his head hanging down over the car door, as the tramp got in behind the wheel and started off, up the road in the direction I had come from.

When there had been any strength in her again, and she had been sure that he was gone, she had arisen from her concealment. She had gone back and got her coat, and climbed out on the road. She had gone on up it, finding no houses, meeting no one, exhausted, terrified, and frantic, till my headlights had come around the rock, and she had flagged me.

That was all. That was all at the time then. St. Erme had been struck down by the tramp, perhaps with a tire iron or crank, and knocked unconscious, she thought. Perhaps he had suffered a cracked skull, she was afraid. That was terrible enough to think about. She had not thought of the knife then. She did not think to mention it until later.

So that was all she had to tell me. An assault on her fiancé, and their car stolen, with him in it. Yet made a little nightmarish by her terror. By the terror that was still in her, underneath, of her pursuit by Corkscrew through the darkening woods.

Three quarters of a mile or so down the road I found a place to turn around, where twelve or fifteen feet of level ground extended beyond the road edge on the left, carpeted with grasses and black-eyed Susans, and bordered by an old rotted worm fence, beyond which was a deep sloping woods, with a glimpse of dark starlit water down through trees.

"There's the lake we were going to picnic by!" she said.

"This is the very place we left the car. We were down there by the water when I saw him spying on us. Inis ran after him up here. I was hiding all through the woods, behind every rock and bush, while he hunted me."

I took my flashlight from the glove compartment and got out, before I had turned around, looking the ground over. I could still see the tire tracks in the flattened grasses where the heavy car had been driven off the road, and had then gone on.

There was some dark wetness glistening on the weed stems beside the right-hand tire imprints, those nearer to the fence and woods. It wasn't crankcase oil. I stooped and felt the ground with my palm. A larger quantity of blood had been spilled here than a man could lose from a nosebleed or a cracked head. A larger quantity than he could lose unless an artery was severed and spurting out.

For a moment, squatting on my haunches, I held my palm in front of me, away from my knees, thinking of that other moment, in the twilight an hour before, when I had heard the croaking in the weeds beside the road, and had found that blue hat with the saw-tooth brim. That damned remembered hat.

I wiped my hand on clean grasses. But it was more than my hand, I felt, that I had put in murder. It was all around me. Up to my neck.

I got into my car again, and turned it around, and brought her back to MacComerou's here, where the police were already waiting.

If St. Erme's right hand was there at that time, among the weedy flowers and grasses on the road edge overlooking Dead Bridegroom's Pond, I didn't see it. I wasn't looking for it, it is true. I had no way of knowing that it would be missing when he should be found. Lieutenant Rosenblatt has sent down a couple of the troopers now and some of the posse men to search all that spot of ground and the woods adjacent. But I do not believe they will find it there.

It was such a damned ordinary and commonplace crime, on the face of it—that first murder of the demon.

It fits an almost tediously banal police pattern, as I understand it. A moronic hitchhiker, having been picked up on the road, yields to a sudden impulse, when the opportunity is given to him, and steals his accommodating driver's car and possessions, with murder as a mere casual incident to the theft. Not realizing the certainty, after a few miles, or at the most a few hundreds, of being caught.

Every year, in almost every state of the Union, during ordinary times—and often enough still even in these gasless days, it seems—some man is sent to the chair or the gas chamber for a stupid, unpremeditated murder of that sort. There is nothing in the picture of Corkscrew to differentiate him from any other such moronic, almost incidental killer, it would seem, except that afterward he made a supernormally cunning effort to conceal what he had done. And that, when he did not succeed in concealing it completely, he killed again.

And, most of all, that he hasn't yet been caught.

I don't believe that Rosenblatt was quite satisfied, from the beginning, with the picture, by the nature of the questions he asked. A slow and stolid policeman, with a mind a little dull and trivial, but very persistent and tenacious. I can see him yet, sitting at the marble-topped table in the living room here, with his wrinkled bulldog face hunched solidly on his burly neckless shoulders, with his forearms planted, making his inquiries with a corrugated brow, and carefully setting down the answers that he got, in his small round handwriting, on the pages of his fat dogeared notebook.

Going back into Elinor Darrie's life, and into St. Erme's, and into everyone's who might have remotely touched them, to try to find a previous trace of that fantastic killer.

Q. [To Miss Darrie] Tell me all about yourself, Miss Darrie. Where you came from. Where you live. How long you and Mr. St. Erme have known each other. What other men you know, or have known.
A. My name is Elinor Darrie. I am nineteen years old. I come from Spardersburg, Pa. I work in the Riddle Insurance Agency in New York. I live at 514 West Eleventh, in the Village. . . .

I have known her only these few hours of the years of her life, yet I think I am acquainted with all the details about her. She was born in her little Pennsylvania town, the daughter of a country newspaper editor and of a mother who had been a schoolteacher. Her parents died together in a fire when she was very small, and she was brought up by her old Amish grandmother. She went to high school, and then stayed home, taking care of her grandmother, and secretly trying to write stories. She is romantic and imaginative, and always wanted to be a writer, as do many lonely children.

Her grandmother died this spring, leaving her only the mortgaged house they lived in. The local real-estate and insurance man who was her executor succeeded in selling it for her for a small sum, and with the money she came to New York, where she took a tiny studio apartment in Greenwich Village, and got her receptionist's job with the Riddle Agency through a newspaper advertisement. Living in the Village was what she had always dreamed of doing—the name symbolizing to her a world of freedom and romance, of glamour and art, as it still does to many small-town girls. Though I live in it myself and hadn't even known that I was living in it, until she called it that; and all it is is just another bunch of buildings, shops, eating places, and dirty streets.

She had never been out of Spardersburg before. Her grandmother had brought her up quite strictly, without even the ordinary social freedoms which most girls enjoy. She had had no attachments or love affairs, not even a high-school sweetheart, before she met St. Erme. It would be hard to see why not, perhaps, except that she was brought up to be afraid of boys and men. Which is something that the male animal is apt to sense in a girl. And though to a few it may be a hunting call, it tends to keep most of them away from her.

There is nothing in her past life, then, to indicate even remotely that anyone might have been impelled to do murder because of a passional jealousy over her. She had never met Corkscrew before today, to the best of her knowledge.

Q. 514 West Eleventh? That is near where Dr. Riddle lives, is it not, Miss Darrie?

A. [By Dr. Riddle] It is right across the street. However, Miss Darrie and I had never happened to run into each other before tonight.

Q. [To Dr. Riddle] Thank you, Doctor. The Riddle Insurance Agency, where Miss Darrie has been employed—you don't happen to know anything about it, I suppose?

A. It is owned by a second cousin of my father's, I believe, Paul Riddle. I don't know him, but I believe his business reputation is quite sound. I have no connection with his firm myself.

Q. Surgeons' and Physicians', and St. John's Medical, are your connections, Doctor?

A. That is right.

Q. A specialist in surgery?

A. In brain surgery, chiefly. Of course I sometimes do other things. . . .

Question. [To Miss Darrie] Tell me all about Mr. St. Erme, Miss Darrie. Where he came from, and what his business was. What physical or personality pecu-

liarities he had. Was Inis St. Erme his full name, by
the way, or did he have a middle name?

A. That was his middle name. His first initial was
S—S. Inis. But he only used it as a signature, I think.
On his insurance application, and the check he drew
at the bank this morning. I don't know what it stood
for. He always liked to be called just Inis. It was his
mother's family name, I think, a Scots name. His last
name was French. He came from somewhere in the
Middle West, from Oklahoma. . . .

She met St. Erme for the first time a couple of months
ago when he dropped in to obtain some business insurance
at her office, to which he had been recommended.

He was a tall, black-eyed man, thirty-three years old, according to the data he gave on his insurance application. He
had dark wavy hair which he wore rather long, and a white,
somewhat diffident smile. He was well dressed, and wore a
heavy seal ring on his right hand.

He came from Texas and Oklahoma, the son of a wild-
catting oil man of French-Canadian ancestry, she learned
after she had got to know him, who had made pots of money, and squandered and tossed them away, and had made
pots more—and who had had the good luck to die, so far
as his son was concerned, at a time when the pots were full.
On his mother's side he had some Scots and Indian blood,
he had said. . . . Elinor had rather got the idea, without
any particular reason for having it, that his first name might

have been an Indian one which he didn't like, and that that was the reason he never told her what it was—some name such as Sachem or Seminole.

Like her, he had not been in New York long, and had no circle of friends, which was in itself a bond between them from the start. His only acquaintances, so far as she knew, were his lawyers and brokers, whom he had sometimes referred to, and one or two business associates whose names she knew. His business was that of an entrepreneur and investor, and also she had got the idea that he played the market at times, when there was a profit to be made in doing it.

He had never gone around with a girl before her, he told her. He had always been a little afraid of them, he said. But she had a feeling that actually it had been because women didn't appeal to him, in general—he had none of the ogling of each passing shape and face which afflicts so many men, perhaps most men, even when in love and on the verge of marriage. His interests since he had been a boy had been mostly financial. His diversions were chiefly newspaper reading and movie-going, with a preference for horse operas and adventure films having a minimum of girls and love interest. He had little interest in literature or books. His eyes quite possibly would have kept him from much reading, even if he had cared for it, she thought.

St. Erme's eyes were apparently quite bad. It was a handicap not obvious, however, since he wore contact lenses, and had learned how to get around. He never mentioned it himself. Elinor had known him three or four weeks before she realized that he wore glasses at all. A glint of candlelight in a restaurant had been what had told her then, catching his eyes at an angle, and turning them for an instant to blank, shining glass. She had remembered, when she realized he wore glasses, that occasionally she had noticed him stumbling over some small unexpected obstacle, such as a street curb that was a little high, or a hassock in her apartment that might have been moved out of its customary place—things that, even without glasses, were visible enough to her.

She had never spoken to him about his eyes, after she had discovered it, however. She had always suffered from a consciousness of her own nearsightedness, though it was nothing in comparison to his. But she was more thoughtful of him because of it. . . .

That endeavor on St. Erme's part to conceal the fact that his eyes were not normal, even from the girl he loved, would seem to indicate a rather juvenile vanity in him, which does not fit in with the other details she supplied of him as a mature and solid man of business, who should have been beyond small shams and pretenses. Yet some men are vain about one small particular thing, and nothing else. There are generals who wear corsets.

And no man—no man living—makes a completely perfect picture. Even less the dead.

Lack of perfect eyesight is no barrier to obtaining life insurance, anyway. The examining doctors aren't interested in whether a man's eyes are jellybeans or glass. They are interested in his heart and kidneys. If they concern themselves with his eyes at all, it is only to peer back of them with an ophthalmoscope at the blood vessels in the fundus, trying to guess from their appearance how long he will live. Though that is a thing which even the best can't answer.

I never saw St. Erme alive myself. These details about him are what Elinor Darrie told me, as I drove up the road with her from Dead Bridegroom's Pond, and what she told in fuller detail in answer to Lieutenant Rosenblatt's questions later.

Q. [To Miss Darrie] If anyone—if this man that we are calling Corkscrew—had known that Mr. St. Erme was nearly blind, before he hailed you, it might have been useful to him. But you had never mentioned Mr. St. Erme's handicap to anyone, had you, Miss Darrie?
A. That would have been terrible. I mean Inis didn't want even me to know anything about it, I felt. I would have thought it terrible to have told other people about it. I never discussed anything about him with anybody.
Q. Never with anybody?
A. Well, I told Mr. Riddle, Mr. Paul Riddle, my boss, that I thought Mr. St. Erme was nice. But I never discussed him with anybody.
Q. Who was the doctor who examined Mr. St. Erme for his insurance?
A. Dr. Burnstetter. He has been doing that work for Mr. Riddle's company for forty years.

Q. Did he notice that Mr. St. Erme's eyes were so bad, himself?

A. He didn't mention it on his report form, I don't think. Of course, he wouldn't have made a special notation of it, unless it had something to do with an examinee's general health. And Inis was quite healthy, really. Except for his eyes, he had nothing wrong.

Q. Even though he didn't mention it in his report, Dr. Burnstetter could have told about Mr. St. Erme's handicap to someone else, couldn't he?

A. [By Dr. Riddle] That's a ridiculous assumption, Lieutenant. Physicians don't go around blabbing about their patient's handicaps or defects. For one thing, they know too many different kinds to make any particular individual's seem interesting. For another, it's against their oath.

Q. But they might say something to another physician, mightn't they, Doctor?

A. If there were anything medically unusual in the case.

Q. Do you happen to know Dr. Burnstetter yourself, Doctor?

A. No, I've never heard of him. Of course he might belong to some medical society that I belong to, and I may have met and conversed with him at some meeting. But I have no recollection of him, nor of anything we may have discussed. He never discussed his examinees' myopia with me, to the best of my knowledge. I never heard of St. Erme.

Q. [To Miss Darrie] Could you tell me something about the business for which Mr. St. Erme got his insurance? Who might benefit by his death?

A. [By Miss Darrie] It was some kind of business that he was in with Mr. Dexter, who owns a garage. An inventing business. Mr. Dexter wouldn't benefit, in any way important. Inis was going to make millions for him. . . .

The business for which St. Erme had wanted to insure his life was a side line in which he had become interested. He had discovered a garage owner, A. M. Dexter, owning a place on West Fourteenth, who was one of these gadgetmakers and mechanical geniuses, and had formed a grub-staking partnership with Dexter to develop and exploit some of his inventions.

The situation of Dexter, when St. Erme found him, was this: that he was a man of considerable native ingenuity and creative imagination, but was impractical, and without any business sense. He would work on some device till he had got it toward the final stage, and then would lose interest in it; or would perhaps find himself tied up for lack of a few hundred dollars of necessary capital to make a working model, and would turn in a frenzy of fresh enthusiasm to something else, and go through the same whole bootless process again.

Dexter had never patented anything. He had never actually quite perfected anything. He had never thought of any of his inventions from the utilitarian and commercial point of view, in terms of money that might be made from them and the uses to which they might be put. He was just a puttering, baldheaded, grease-stained, middle-aged mechanic, essentially, who liked to tinker with odd devices for the fun of it, owning a small business that was always on the verge of bankruptcy. Yet when St. Erme had looked his shop over, he had found that Dexter had on the ways no less than half a dozen devices of great promise, including an adaption of the radar principle for perceiving objects under water, a television walkie-talkie of light and inexpensive construction, and a method of producing a rubber substitute from coalmine refuse culm at a cost which St. Erme estimated would be no more than a fraction of a cent a pound.

St. Erme did not claim to be a technical man. Yet it would require no great amount of mechanical understanding to see that if even one of those inventions was perfected, and proved practicable, it would be worth almost any sum, quite apart from any patriotic consideration of the importance, to the nation at war, of some of those devices for military use. By subsidizing Dexter with the necessary money for materials and models, St. Erme would share fifty-fifty in any profits. At the worst, if all those devices should prove to be only a gadget-maker's dreams, he would not stand to lose very much.

He had signed partnership papers with Dexter, and had put Dexter on a regular drawing account in lieu of salary, with regulated and business methods of work. He had wanted to insure that Dexter would be able to continue, in case of his own death.

He might have set aside twenty-five thousand dollars in a special bank account for that purpose. But it was simpler to make the provision in the form of insurance, without putting up the cash where it might be tied up in litigation, in case Dexter should prove to be only a crazy dreamer or even a chiseling fraud. The insurance, in that case, could merely be allowed to lapse.

It was the way his lawyers had advised him to handle it.

Dexter, the garage man, had no knowledge that St. Erme had taken out any insurance in his favor, it would seem, from his conversation when old MacComerou called him up at dusk.

Dexter did not seem to know a great deal about St. Erme in any way. He did not even know where St. Erme lived in New York. He didn't know Elinor Darrie's name, and wasn't aware that St. Erme was being married. He had even forgotten that St. Erme had borrowed his car, until reminded of it. He was working on an invention and couldn't be bothered.

"Young St. Erme?" he told MacComerou, in his dry rasping voice which I couldn't help but overhear. "Certainly I know him, Professor. He's backing me. He's got a lot of money. A fine young fellow, straight as a die, with a smart head on his shoulders. We're going to make ten million dollars, he says, when I get a gadget finished that I'm working on. . . .

"No, I haven't seen him today, that I remember. He lives at some hotel here in New York, I've forgotten the name of it. He has a girl, I think, who might know. He called me up last night to borrow my sport touring job for a few days, come to think of it. He wanted to go some place with his girl.

"Where did you say you're calling from, Professor? Up in the Berkshires in north Connecticut? That does sound like my job you saw go by. XL 465-297's the license number, if you happened to get a look at it. I gave him the loan of it. His girl was going to drive it. That's all I know about it. I hope there's nothing wrong. If anything happened to the boy, I'd be in a bad way. Excuse me, I've got something boiling on the stove that's liable to blow up on me. Can you call me up some other time, Professor?"

And click! A hundred miles away down in New York, Inis St. Erme's gadgetmaking partner had hung up dryly.

That was within an hour, at most, of the time of St. Erme's murder. Before it was more than a shadowy and intangible projection that something dark and diabolic might have happened to him. He might not even have been dead at that moment, it was possible. Down there on the Swamp Road a mile away, still alive and still all too terribly aware, with crazy laughing little Corkscrew and his knife.

That scene keeps coming back to me—that scene at twilight when I first came here, looking for some help in getting started, with my car stalled at the entrance to the Swamp Road.

The voices of the locusts come back to me, and the gray bird fluttering frantically in my face, and the sound, like a great frog croaking in the weedy ditch, there had been as I came down the road, and that hat which I had found, that damned blue mutilated hat. There was something in all of it that troubled old MacComerou. There was something in the picture that he knew could not be right.

There were only the two of us around the place here, then. No one knew yet that murder had been done. St. Erme wasn't even a name to me. Corkscrew not even a phantom. But old MacComerou had seen that gray car rushing by, and I had not seen it. And he knew the picture wasn't right.

The question is, what train of thought had started in his keen old brain, which impelled him to call up Dexter? There was something about that car which he wanted answered. I can see him yet, standing at the phone out in the kitchen, still in his gardening shorts and moccasins, with dirt and sweat over him, gaunt and bent-shouldered, a gray furze on his pale chest, laying a big silver watch down deliberately on the slanting phone-box ledge beneath the mouthpiece before thumbing through his black book for Dexter's number, then ringing the crank with a long white arm like a peeled white stick, and asking for toll operator, which is Connecticutese for long distance.

Putting his questions to Dexter, when he had got him,

with meditative deliberation, still thumbing through his black book while he listened to Dexter's rasping answers. Perhaps looking for other numbers to call up, if the car had not been Dexter's. With his big old brain working beneath his flat bald skull, and his shrewd faded blue eyes that knew too much of murder.

Yet whatever the thought in old MacComerou's mind, I missed it. He seemed satisfied with the information Dexter gave him, anyway, as he turned and looked at me. There is nothing in the picture that I can see, nothing whatever, to connect St. Erme's doodling garage-man partner with red-eyed little Corkscrew.

There is nothing to connect him with anyone. He appears to have come from limbo, and to have vanished the same way. The problem must be approached from the beginning. To trace back, if possible, at what moment he first appeared upon the scene—that red-eyed wedding guest.

Q. [To Miss Darrie] When did you and Mr. St. Erme first decide on your wedding journey today, Miss Darrie? How large a sum of money was he carrying with him? Who knew where you were going?

A. We decided to get married only yesterday at lunch. I don't know just how much money Inis had with him, but it was at least twenty-five hundred dollars. No one knew where we were going. We didn't know ourselves. . . .

It had been, it seemed, only about thirty hours before I met her there on the road that she and St. Erme had decided to get married.

They had been having lunch together at a little place near her office. A place where people ate outdoors, in a Spanish patio beside a fountain, with caged birds singing; and it was a bright sunshiny day in August, and they had known each other nearly two months.

St. Erme had not spoken of marriage to her before. It had been something that had not been in her own mind at all, at the moment. She might have thought of it subconsciously, at different times, as a possible eventual culmination of their acquaintance, as a girl does, but not as anything immediate or even necessarily very probable. There was the difference in their ages and their stations. It was only something which after a year or so he might propose, if he still continued to see her and find her company pleasant; and which she might consider then.

She had never had a man in love with her before. She had not realized that he was.

But this was New York, not Spardersburg, and St. Erme was a man of decision, not a mooning boy. They were both alone in New York and the world, and only themselves mattered. In the time that they had known each other they had dined together, and had gone to movies together, to the Central Park Zoo and Radio City, and had ridden on the ferry to Staten Island and listened to concerts at the Stadium, and done all those other things together which can be done during a summer in New York. St. Erme had learned about her all that there was to know, perhaps; and she about him all that she would ever know. And so it might as well be now.

He had set down his demitasse and tossed his crumpled napkin on the table.

"Let's get married," he had said to her, smiling at her with his diffident white smile, his black eyes crinkled. "Let's get married right away today."

All that she would ever know. But as much, perhaps, as most girls know about the man they marry. A girl must take the unread pages on faith, or the whole thing is nothing.

"Why not?" she had replied, her heart beating.

And that's the way it's agreed, after luncheon on a bright summer day, in a patio with birds singing and a fountain playing, or in some other pleasant setting, by an exchange of casual words, when there are no relatives from whom to obtain permission or friends to be informed, but only the two of them in the whole world, and wanting life to be like this moment always.

St. Erme had summoned the check; and on the way out they had stopped at a telephone booth, where she had called up her office, saying that she would not be back that afternoon. She had already had a tentative permission to take the afternoon off, if she should want to for shopping. Without any more preliminaries than that, without any plan, they had taken the near-by subway down to City Hall.

But New York State has a three-day law, they had learned at the license bureau. St. Erme had thought then of Connecticut, as many people do. Even people who have lived in New York all their lives are apt to think of Connecticut as an elopers' paradise, perhaps because Greenwich is the first railroad station in that state, and its name is confused with Gretna Green. Though actually Connecticut has had a five-day law for a long time.

St. Erme and she didn't know about that, however. When they learned about the New York law, he had thought of Connecticut. It was too late to go there that day, though. They would have to put it off till the next. It had occurred to him that they might go by car, and they could then go on up, making a honeymoon of it, to Maine or Montreal.

St. Erme hadn't brought his own car East with him, with his chauffeur now in the army and the gas situation what it was. Rather than trying to rent a limousine with chauffeur, though, he would see if he could get a car from Dexter for her to drive.

He didn't say that his eyes were the reason he didn't drive. He merely explained it to her, with his curious small vanity, that he had never had the time to learn. But she could drive, of course, having always driven her grandmother's car. Even old Amish ladies, who think that modern inventions like buttons are all sinful, used to like to sit spread out on the back seat of a sedan in their black bombazines, with their hands folded on their laps, and watch the trees and houses and telephone poles and cows go past, like everyone else, in the days of rubber and gas.

Driving a car was something that she had always enjoyed doing. She had even got a New York driver's license, at a cost of a dollar and a half for three years, on first coming to the city, with the idea of some day perhaps sending for the old sedan. However, its tires were gone; and her grandmother's executor back in Spardersburg had sold it for seventy-five dollars. So that part of her life was already over.

St. Erme had called up Dexter during dinner, when they had decided on it, and had secured the use of Dexter's gray Cadillac sport touring for as long as he might want it. A colored boy from Dexter's garage had delivered it to her apartment the next morning, and had then driven around the block with her a few times, until she had got the feel of it.

"Should I give you a receipt, or is Mr. St. Erme's name sufficient?" she asked the boy, when she had returned him to the garage to which he directed her, a few blocks distant.

The boy shook his head.

"Mr. Dexter just gave word to the night man to deliver it to you all this morning. He didn't say anything about wanting a receipt."

"Perhaps Mr. Dexter would like to pass on me himself before I take it, if he's not too busy," she had said. "It's a perfectly beautiful car, and I wouldn't want him to be worrying that I might wreck it."

"Mr. Dexter ain't been in this morning yet, I don't

think," said the boy. "He ain't always. Just remember that your gear shift's on the steering post, and you don't have to keep reaching down around your knees. I reckon you aren't any crazy driver, and won't hurt it. You aren't going to steal it, neither, I don't guess. Nobody wouldn't get nowhere very far with it if they did. Might as well try to steal a fire engine. Just listen to that horn."

He pressed a high-pitched wailing blast from the button, as he got out.

"That says, 'Here I come like a big gray ball of fire! Get out of my way, all you good-for-nothing onery little puddle-jumpers!'" he told her with a grin. "Some day I'd sure like to have a car like her myself. Boy, I'd sure make their eyes bug out."

A short fat bald white man in a grease-stained monkey suit had come out of the garage doors at the blast.

"Miss Burry?" he said, wiping his hands on waste. "Mr. Dexter just called up to ask if you had got it. He wasn't sure if he had got the address right. But I see he did."

"Miss Darrie," she said. "I thought perhaps you were Mr. Dexter. Thank him for me, anyway, and for Mr. St. Erme."

"Me Dexter?" he said with a laugh. "Good Lord, I'm just Gus. Dexter is twice as big, twice as homely, and twice as dumb. Thank him for who? Mr. Saturn? Never mind, I guess Mr. Dexter knows who it is, anyway. He wouldn't let anybody use that car unless he thought a lot of them. Your gas tank's filled up, and the coupon book's in the glove compartment. C to H are still good. You must be planning to drive quite a ways. Are you going on a honeymoon or something?"

"More or less," she told him, flushing.

"I've been all through that myself," he said. "Nine kids of my own now. It won't be long till you're like I am. Good luck to you."

She had picked up St. Erme at his hotel. He lived at the President in midtown, not far from her office. They had stopped at his bank in the neighborhood for him to get a check cashed; and since the bank was also hers, she wanted at the same time to draw out five or ten dollars herself—she had, as usual, only a little silver in her purse. They had left the car outside the bank, with their bags in it.

The bank had been normally filled with customers for a Wednesday middle morning in a midtown bank—no more and no less. Perhaps fifty customers, perhaps a hundred. She had stood beside St. Erme at the counter by the front window, filling in the date and signature on her own little check, thinking with a feeling of fatality that it was the last time she would ever sign herself Elinor Darrie, and debating how much to make it out for, while he had been writing his.

"Shall I make it for ten or fifteen, Inis?" she had asked him doubtfully.

He had smiled at her, with the happiness a man can feel who has a great deal of money, all of which is his to give now to the one loved woman, from this time forth.

"Be extravagant, and make it twenty, my sweet," he had told her, amused by the smallness of her financial transactions.

He had laid his hand on her arm abruptly then.

"The car!" he said, with a sharpness in his voice which startled her.

"What's happened to it?" she asked him, staring out the window. "It's still there."

"A fellow crossing the street just back of it stopped and looked at it," he said, relaxing. "It looked for a moment as if he might be reaching into it. But he seems to have gone on."

"You took out the keys, didn't you?" she said. "You said you would."

"I was thinking of the bags," he told her grimly. "I've got Dexter's rubber formula in mine, for study. It's this damned war. It makes us all spy-crazy. He was probably just a casual pedestrian, admiring the bus. But I think one of us had better keep an eye on it, just for luck."

She had given him her check to cash along with his while she had remained to watch the bags. She hadn't seen how much his had been for at the time he had been making it out. She had assumed perhaps something like a hundred dollars. When he had reached the teller's window in his line, she had seen him smiling back at her, however. She had thought that he wanted to say something to her. Out in front a patrolman had passed by the car, looking it over; and he seemed solid and substantial, so she thought she could leave the front window for a moment. Going back to join Inis, she had been in time to see the teller counting out a sheaf of fifty-dollar bills to him as she came up.

"I asked one of the bank guards to keep an eye on the car," he told her. "We're all set now."

The teller—a sandy young man with hangdog eyes, who had tried once or twice, she thought, to address a flirtatious remark to her when she had come in with her firm's deposits or her own modest salary—nodded moodily to her behind his wicket.

"Fifty fifties," he said. "Good morning, Miss Darrie. You're undertaking a big new venture, I understand. I wish you luck with it, and much increase and prosperity."

She felt her face warm, as it had been at the garage when the man named Gus had spoken of his nine children. She walked away with her hand in Inis's arm, out to the car.

"Why does everyone always leer at you when they know you're going to get married?" she said. "I rather wish you hadn't had to tell him, Inis. Or anybody. I mean, until we are."

He smiled at her with wrinkling eyes.

"I didn't tell him," he said. "He just guessed it, it seems, my sweet. He's the one you told me has been casting sheep's eyes at you, isn't he? Young Sawyer. I'd forgotten about it. He's a fairly decent young sprig, though. Perhaps we can have him to dinner and a show sometime, with some nice girl or other, when we get back."

"Why," she asked him, "should we? I've hardly ever spoken more than a word to him, Inis. I wouldn't even know his name, except for the sign on his counter. Why on earth should we have him to dinner and a show?"

"I just thought that you might like to look forward to having a circle of friends of your own age," he said tenderly. "Social life. Entertaining. Being a hostess, and things like that. I don't want you to feel in any way that, in marrying me, your life is ended. But it doesn't make any difference about Sawyer, if you don't like him."

"It isn't that I dislike him," she said. "He just seems like a nonentity to me."

"He is, of course," St. Erme agreed.

He passed her a bill, putting his bulging wallet away in his breast pocket, outside the bank door.

"Put it in your purse," he said.

"Fifty dollars!" she exclaimed, with a breathless exclamation of pleasure, so that one or two passing pedestrians turned to look at her happy face. "Why, I only made out my check for twenty, Inis."

"I tore up your silly little check, sweet," he told her, a little bored. "Your money's no good any more. Try and use it."

"But what on earth could I do with all this money?" she said, as she put it carefully away. "I've never had so much before."

"All that money," he smiled at her. "I don't know. What can you do with fifty dollars? Treat yourself to a lunch at the

Waldorf sometime, or buy yourself a crazy little hat. Or how much do crazy little hats cost?"

"Not that much, I hope," she said.

For a moment they stood smiling at each other, out of sheer happiness over nothing. That she thought fifty dollars was much money. That he didn't even know the cost of women's hats.

The patrolman was still by the car when they crossed the sidewalk and got into it. Nothing had been touched, apparently. Nothing was missing. The patrolman smiled at them. Wealth, youth, beauty, and carefree joy. A sunlit summer day. The world before them. A fine big shiny powerful car with its top down, smoke gray, with blood-red cushions. No doubt he envied them. He would have liked to get in himself, and go riding off with them, to the world's end. But he had his job, to watch out for thieves and all other kinds of criminals, and he could not afford to leave it, even if they had asked him to come along.

With the shadow of a smiling nod he turned away, to go about his business. . . .

It was not until they had gone several blocks from the bank that Elinor realized, with a belated arithmetical computation, the size of the check that Inis must have drawn. Fifty fifties—twenty-five hundred dollars which he had with him in his purse, plus whatever else he might have had before, and less only the bill that he had handed to her. It seemed an appalling sum to her, merely to be carrying around in one's pocket for day-by-day expenditures, even if they should be gone a month.

But his standards of money weren't the same as hers, she realized. She would have to get used to many different values of all sorts, from the small and narrow ones she had always known.

She had already phoned her office, earlier in the morning, to say that she would begin her vacation which had been offered her, if still convenient; though without telling what she was doing.

There had been that disappointment the previous afternoon at the license bureau and she had been glad that she had not told anybody then. Perhaps there was some subliminal uncertainty, some shadowy inquietude still lurking below the threshold of her mind, that another unforeseen event might again occur to thwart them. A presentiment, however formless and dim, of some dark opposing hand rising up against her and Inis.

Yet perhaps that is only hindsight on her part—she wasn't sure, when she spoke of it to me. She told no one, anyway; and St. Erme had no one whom he needed to notify. There was no one who knew that they were going anywhere, except Dexter and the colored boy who had delivered the car to her, and Gus at the garage. And Dexter or the colored boy or Gus had not known where they were going, or what roads they would take.

They didn't know themselves. They had no planned itinerary. They just started rolling, up the Grand Concourse, and out along the Bronx River Parkway; and then taking this road and that bearing in the general directions east and north, as a way might appeal to one or the other of them, knowing they would find Connecticut at the end, just where God had planted it, by and by. There isn't much traffic on any road these days, and they had the way mostly to themselves. They passed only a few cars heading the opposite direction, and there was only an occasional one ahead of them or behind them, going the same way.

Assuming that someone had been standing in line behind St. Erme at the teller's window in the bank, and had seen him cashing his big check, and had tried to follow them, he must have been driving an invisible car, paler than any smoke, transparent as glass. For there were miles and miles of bright sunlit concrete highway, and miles and miles of shady winding macadam side roads, where there was no other car in sight at all. . . .

They stopped for a late luncheon somewhere still in New York State, at a roadside teahouse built over a water mill, overlooking a pretty reservoir lake. There was only one other customer, an old, old man with a bald shiny head and toothless gums, who sat across the dining room from them, out of earshot, munching his soft food, and who paid no attention to them. Elinor remembers him because he was such a funny-looking old man, and she teased Inis that he would look like that someday, and asked if he would still expect her to love him. It seemed a joke to her that Inis and she would ever really be old. Age happened to other people, but it would never happen to them. They would always be in summertime and in love, and this day would last forever.

But Inis had taken it a little seriously, and had asked if he seemed old to her. He had—though she did not tell him— seemed a great deal older than she when she had first met him, with the crinkles about his eyes, and the air of hidden depth and experience a man gets from living. But she had forgotten the difference in their ages now, to a large extent. . . . Her joking remark about the old man had cast a shadow on the moment, and the bright day seemed darker, and the sound of the purling water mill beneath their feet like the sound of rain on graves or like a weeping. There had come a dark invisible shadow between them at the table; and she had known that she, too, would someday be old; and that before that day came, even, she would be without Inis. Though how soon, she did not know.

The old man left the teahouse before they did, and went off in his car another way. There was no one who followed them from there.

There is no trace of Corkscrew yet that I can see.

It was after half-past three when they reached Danbury, over the line in Connecticut. They learned about the five-day law there, and learned also that Massachusetts to the north had a three-day law, and that the nearest place where they could get married without delay was Vermont.

They sat down in a booth in a little stationery and ice-cream store, and talked it over. It was too late to get to Vermont that day. It seemed to Elinor, and it may have seemed to Inis, that there was some malignant fate opposing them. That an invisible hand had risen up against them, blocking them off.

If they went back, it would take the bloom off the whole thing. The hour, the mood, might never come again. Never the time and the place. There would always be between them a sense of frustration and retreat—of postponement for a few days more, and a few weeks, and perhaps forever. Yet to stop at some hotel overnight, even with all due circumspection, even though being married tomorrow, was something of which she could not conceive. Greenwich Village had not gone that deep with her. Behind her was her old Amish grandmother and all the strict training and deep instincts of her life.

Inis had not liked the thought particularly, either. He had his own sense of reticence, his distaste of being a common show. The picture was offensive to him, as well—of going to a desk and registering, either as man and wife or under their own names, demanding separate rooms, before the eyes of the lobby loungers and the bellboys' curious smirks, while the clerk turned the book around, and read it with a slow fish-eye. He had sat brooding, drumming his brown fingers on the booth table, a little dispirited that she should have suggested going back, and trying to think what they might do.

He had brightened then, with his white smile flashing, suddenly remembering old John R. Buchanan, the steel king, the President's special adviser and one of the great men of the country, whose big summer estate was up near Burlington, just over the border in Vermont. Old John R. Buchanan had been his father's closest friend, and would be more than glad to have them as his guests.

It was too late to reach old John's place in Burlington before one or two o'clock tonight, an hour which would find the whole household dead. But if they made the trip at a leisurely pace, taking a good time out for supper, and stopping for coffee at lunch wagons in Pittsfield and other towns en route, they could reach the Buchanan place around six or seven in the morning, when some of the house servants would be up. They could catch a short sleep there finally, and be on hand when the license office opened up, with nothing more to stop them.

More than just providing them with a place to sleep, old John Buchanan would probably want to arrange a wedding party for them in grand style. What Inis remembered in addition was that the old man had a lakeside cabin farther up in the Green Mountains, a dream place beside a deep blue water, never used, which he had built for his daughter, who had died on the eve of her wedding several years ago, and the first use of which, if he should ever marry, he had promised to old Lefty St. Erme's son and his bride.

He had forgotten about it, because when old John had made the offer he had had no idea of ever marrying. But now, in the stress of fighting against their frustration, against the dark invisible hand held up against them, as she expressed it, he thought of old Buchanan's house and afterward of that beautiful honeymoon place up in the mountains.

Inis had a road map in his pocket, and they had sat there in the booth, picking out the route on it, counting up the distances between towns. And it didn't seem too long and tiresome in prospect, taking it at a leisurely pace, with plenty of stop-offs on the way, and bed at the end. Elinor had felt gay again, infected by his enthusiasm. The way seemed suddenly clear, and there were now a definite shape and plan to what had all been rather planless and shapeless before, their wedding trip. She put from her mind the disquieting thoughts which she had had of turning back.

They would make an adventure of it. They would get picnic supplies here in Danbury, and stop at some pretty spot along the way for supper, perhaps beside a secluded lake where they could have a swim, building a fire afterward and watching the shadows of the flames while the night deepened and the stars came out, lingering until the embers died; and then going on, drifting up through the hills in the warm starlighted darkness, with those stops at the lighted lunch wagons in the little sleeping towns, and on again, while the night faded, and the pearl dawn came, and the pink dawn. And so they would be there at the end, still fresh, still eager, no more tired than from a night of dancing, ready for buckwheat cakes and Vermont sirup and sausages and bed. And after they had slept, they would be married in the great

Buchanan drawing room, with flowers and organ music and a wedding cake, and perhaps an heirloom gown lent by Mrs. Buchanan, and old John himself to give her away; and all those other things which a girl dreams of for her wedding, even though she is without any family of her own and is getting married rather suddenly, on the spur of the moment, without any trousseau or any plans. And afterward they would go up to that paradisiac lakeside cabin in the hills.

And so their honeymoon life together would begin, and go on and on. With never a dark invisible hand rising up against them. . . .

Inis St. Erme did not know, of course. He had no way of knowing. It was just a macabre coincidence that it had suddenly occurred to him that old John R. Buchanan had his summer place near Burlington. But it is a little disquieting to realize that he had planned to take his young bride to a dead man's house. For at that very hour yesterday afternoon when they sat making their bright plans in the little ice-cream parlor in Danbury—though it is a matter quite apart—at his great estate in Burlington, on a white table in a quiet room, old John Buchanan was dying beneath my knife.

Inis and she had gone out of the dark little stationery and ice-cream parlor, and had found a chain grocery next door, where they loaded up with provisions.

There was that sense of an unduplicable experience, the first grocery-buying together, and St. Erme had found pleasure in ordering quantities of everything he saw, with a lordly hand—enough food, it seemed to Elinor, to have lasted the two of them a month, though she, thriftier and more housewifely-wise, would have restrained him. For the rationed commodities, she had her own cards with her in her purse, providently. Inis, a hotel and restaurant liver, had never applied for ration books, and for the moment, until she produced hers, was stumped when he found that they were necessary for cheese and ketchup. . . .

A small detail, ration books. But only one of many. Considered altogether, there were so many small details of which St. Erme did not seem aware. Like the too-high curbs and misplaced hassocks which tripped him up because he had not realized they were there, there were those trivial but obvious things which escaped his mental vision, in the same way, as if he suffered from a blindness in it, as well.

Item, his ignorance of New York marriage laws. Item, his failure to estimate how far they might be able to travel on Dexter's gas coupons, and to lay out their itinerary from the beginning accordingly. Item, his neglect to phone John R. Buchanan's home from Danbury, to give notice that he was coming with his bride. Item, ration books.

Item, his complete lack of concern later—blindest of all—over the appearance of Corkscrew; though that, of course, may have been simply because he could not see.

Yet, taking those items altogether, he was a man peculiarly obfuscated and mentally inept. Only in business did he seem completely intelligent. He must have been intelligent with money. There are men like that, of course.

There was a ten-cent store beyond the grocery; and after they had had their provisions stowed away in the car out front, they went into it. There they bought a griddle, a coffeepot, some paper cups and plates and napkins, a can opener, and some wooden spoons. And there, for a dollar and fifteen cents, they bought the red-handled kitchen bread knife, with its twelve-inch serrated blade. . . .

Corkscrew could have been in the dark little stationery and ice-cream store while they had been laying out their route on the map and calculating their time schedule, of course. He could have been in the next booth to them, eating a dish of chocolate ice cream with slow lickings of his stubbly lips, with little red unblinking eyes upon his spoon, pulling at his torn ear at times, all the while. There is nothing in the picture of him to indicate that he was a man who would not like ice cream.

Nothing in the picture to indicate he wasn't human. That he didn't breathe, that he didn't have to eat and sleep, like any animal. The idea that those grocery supplies which they bought in Danbury and carried with them in the gray Cadillac when they drove out of town had any part in the demon's murder plans seems completely fantastic and unrelated.

Yet I am not sure.

I know the look of him as well as I know my own. Perhaps better. I know his height, his weight, his age, the color of his eyes and hair, the number of his teeth. I know the clothes he wore, to the last item. It seems to me that I know his background, almost, as if I had been brought up next door to him. I know the voice he spoke in. I know his little mannerisms. But I do not know where he came from, and I do not know his name.

I have never laid eyes on him. I feel sure that I shall lay eyes on him before this night is ended. I feel sure that he is somewhere very near me. That is definite. That is the one thing I know. But I do not know yet how I know it. And just that cold feeling in itself does not help me to see him. I have got to dig him out. . . .

They saw him first on the road a little outside of Danbury. He was standing by the roadside, thumbing to go their way. That was the first moment—the very first moment, so far as I can see—that he was visible. That he made an appearance. That a finger can be laid on him at all.

He was a man about forty-five years old. He was a man about five feet, three inches tall. He had a dirty seamy complexion, with a stubble of unshaved bristles growing up to his eyes.

His nose was nondescript—small and rather flat. He had long unkempt hair that was tipped with gray, like the bristles of a badger shaving brush, and raggedly cut about his ears and across the back of his neck, as if with a pair of dull shears ineptly handled. His left ear lobe had been torn or bitten off, giving his face a lopsided look seen from the front—a look a little baffling, of something inexplicably missing, until one realized what it was. His teeth were spaced rather wide apart, and pointed, when he grinned.

He wore a filthy old blue hat, with its brim cut away in saw-tooth scallops all around. He wore a dirty black and white checked sport jacket with a belted back, of shoddy material, with torn elbows, and bereft of buttons, as if it might have been passed on to him by some thrifty housewife who had first cut the buttons off.

He wore a faded green polo shirt, with almost all the coloring washed out of it, unbuttoned at the throat. He wore a garish green and red necktie of ten-cent-store pattern, loosely knotted, with the knot hanging down on his second shirt button—it was the only item of his clothing that seemed new or clean. His heavy corduroy pants were too big around the waist for him, and were gathered in folds about his middle with a broken black trunk strap. They were too long for him as well, and the legs wobbled down their length like the bellows of an accordion, giving an uneven silhouette to the lower half of him, like a man with corkscrew legs.

He might be called Red Eyes, or Clipped Ear, or Saw-tooth just as well, then, from his appearance. But it was because of those ridiculous-looking legs of his that Lieutenant Rosenblatt has named him Corkscrew Legs, or just Corkscrew, tentatively. Until his true name is known.

The late-afternoon sun was at his back. He had some small, gray thing in his arm, which they didn't see till they were almost on him. He had nothing else, no bag, no bundle.

He lifted up his thumb with a grin to them as they came on. He was the little man who was there. The curtain was lifted on his brief but terrible appearance.

I can see them coming on, Elinor and Inis St. Erme, along the late sunlit highway, between the rolling summer meadows and the pleasant wooded hills, in the smoke-gray car with its red leather upholstery, its chromium gleaming, its whitewall tires purring, with its top and windshield down.

I can see them, moneyed and carefree, bright as butterflies beneath the summer sun, on their way to their wedding and honeymoon, and happiness forever after. I can see her with her dark brown hair blowing, her chin up proudly, watching the road through the azure-framed 500 glasses which she needed to use for driving, with her white summer coat open, the wind riffling the collar of her periwinkle-blue dress, with her big emerald ring which St. Erme had given her last night reflecting sunlight on her left hand on the wheel. I can see St. Erme beside her, with his white smile in his brown face, his head bent a little aslant against the breeze, holding his broad-brimmed, fine-textured Panama down on his head, with one arm lifted, and his other arm, in dove-gray gabardine of rippling sheen, lying along the top of the cushions back of her shoulders, a touch of white silk shirt cuff at his wrist, of gold love-knot cuff link, and his massive carved antique gold Florentine ring on his hand.

No, he always wore his Borgia poison ring on his right hand, of course. The ring was on his hand that was holding down his Panama. It was the one thing that wasn't found. But he did have a right hand. It was the one he wore his ring on. He was holding down his hat with it.

That's the picture as I see it, as they came on. It was the picture Corkscrew must have seen, standing beside the road, too.

They weren't going fast, just idling along well below the wartime speed limit, enjoying the wind and sunlight and the sight of the blue hills stretching roll on roll ahead. There was time enough to kill before they reached Vermont. The concrete road was straight and wide. They could see his figure from a distance, and for some little time. Not for a great time, perhaps. But if they were a mile away when they first saw him, they had more than two minutes. If they were only half a mile, they still had more than a minute. Yet it didn't occur to either of them to turn around and speed away.

They couldn't see all the details of him from any distance, of course. And there were some details that Elinor didn't see at once, even when they had stopped beside him and he was getting into their car—details that she absorbed later, more or less subconsciously, as she glanced at him in the rear-view mirror while he was riding in the back seat, and that came back to her in full force as she fled and hid from him in terror and breathless silence during that hour of horror by the black wooded waters of Dead Bridegroom's Pond. As for St. Erme, with his blind eyes, perhaps there were details of Corkscrew which he never did see.

But they both had time enough to see, at least, that he was an extraordinarily repulsive-looking little man.

Repulsive—that was the feeling Elinor Darrie had about him at first sight. A distaste of his sheer dirtiness. A crawling in her skin. But not fear, at first. She hadn't thought of it as fear, anyway.

"Do you see what I see, Inis?" she exclaimed. "That extraordinary little man ahead!"

Inis peered from beneath his flapping hat brim.

"What's so extraordinary about him, sweet?" he said. "He looks like just a tramp to me."

"Everything about him!" she said with vehemence. "He's positively a tramp to end all tramps. Why, he's grinning at us and thumbing us, do you see him, Inis? How ridiculous! He looks as if he actually believes he's going to have us stop and pick him up."

"Maybe he's advertising something," Inis St. Erme said idly. "He does look damned odd, doesn't he? He's got something funny he's holding in his arm. What the devil is it? Like some kind of a gray rag, with something red about it——"

"Why, it's a kitten!" she said. "It's a little gray kitten, with a red mouth!"

She had taken her foot off the accelerator. She did not intend, consciously, to stop. But the thing which Corkscrew was holding in his arm had snared all her attention, with pity and revulsion. With a freezing sense of horror, even, it may be.

"Oh, how dreadful! It's badly hurt!"

St. Erme put forth his hand and turned off the ignition.

She had stalled the engine, and they had stopped. There beside red-eyed little Corkscrew, waiting on the road.

He was no one that St. Erme recognized, then or later, it is evident. No one whom, so far as St. Erme had the slightest idea in his mind, he had ever seen before. He was just a hobo on the road, thumbing for a ride.

Not all the details of him were apparent, instantly. But even if St. Erme had seen every detail, it is improbable that he would have been afraid. St. Erme was not a man who had ever had occasion to feel any particular fear of anything, according to the picture of him. He had money, and so did not know the ordinary human fear of bosses and bill collectors. He was not a soldier, and so had never faced the battle fear. Whatever his religion, it seems improbable that it had given him a fear of hell.

That, essentially, must be considered the key to him. He simply couldn't imagine anything for him to be afraid of. His air of measured diffidence, in itself, can be construed as a kind of hallmark of a profound inner self-assurance, as it often is—an embarrassment of condescension, as when a man feels that he is so intelligent, rich, educated, or otherwise superior that he owes apology to those who must struggle along with so much less.

His background, too, as he sketched it, can be assumed to have given him an additional lack of a salutary sense of fear—the inheritance of a fortune-tossing father, a belief in his lucky star.

A simple lack of fear. Of the fear of hell. It's not the same as—in fact, it precludes—courage. The desperate, sobbing, crazed lion-rabbit courage which makes a man who has it fight with tooth and claw for his life, and fight even when he is half cut in two, and fight till death, and past it.

It's all against the picture that St. Erme had that kind of desperate fighting courage, in the least. Deprived of the self-assurance of his superiority, he might melt like butter. But he was just simply and completely not afraid of the dirty, incredible little man.

"Looking for a lift?" he said amiably. "I guess we have room for you. What the devil happened to your cat?"

Corkscrew had the gray kitten in the crook of his left arm, against his dirty jacket. He was poking at its fur softly and tentatively with his seamy right index finger. It was a fluffy kitten, not many weeks old. Its eyes were still a watery blue. It must have been a pretty little animal once, as most kittens are—as most young living things. But it was filthy now, as filthy as he himself; and there was blood and froth on its muzzle. One of its front paws had been torn off at the shoulder socket, like the leg of a fly, and its head was mangled.

"What happened to it?" Elinor echoed. "Oh, what's happened to it?"

"Found it on the road," said Corkscrew, in a soft quiet voice. "Truck must have run over it, poor little thing."

"Is it dead?"

"It's dead," he said. "End of its troubles."

He lifted it by the scruff, looking at it with his small, inflamed eyes. It had lived out the destiny for which it had been made. He dropped it into the weed-lined ditch beside the road. With a brushing of his palms together, he opened the tonneau door and stepped in.

"Thanks for stopping," he said in his quiet voice. "I kind of figured when I saw you coming that you would. You're my same kind of people. Never used to drive anything but a Cadillac myself. I wouldn't have any other kind of car if you tried to give it to me today. I let two Chevvies and a Dodge pass me by since I've been waiting. But it pays to be particular. I'll just push some of this stuff aside."

"Where are you headed for?" said Inis St. Erme.

"Anywhere," said Corkscrew. "Wherever you're headed for yourselves is all right with me."

He had ensconced himself among the bags and groceries. Elinor looked at Inis a little wryly, but his gaze was blank and unconcerned—almost entranced. She started the car and drove on. Perhaps he had mesmerized them both with his red eyes and his quiet voice, she thought. With his mangled dead gray kitten.

All right, he had that soft, quiet voice. It was one of the chief things that she noticed about him. Its incongruity with his appearance may have emphasized it in her mind. She thought of it as the voice of an educated man, particularly.

The tone of a man's voice has no relation to his education, actually. Valets and vestrymen, bank clerks and burglars, all have quiet voices, even if they have gone no further in school than the fourth elementary grade. While, on the other hand, there are plenty of M.D.'s and LL.D.'s, *summa cum laude* and *causa honoris,* who roar continually like stevedores and bellow like sea elephants. A man who walks heavily by nature talks loudly by nature. A man who walks quietly talks quietly. That is all the tone of a man's voice tells about him.

Yet he may have attended some college somewhere at some time, and may even have been a former member of one of the learned professions, as she felt him to be. Quite possibly there are as many professional men, proportionally, as men of any other classes or categories, among hoboes and derelicts, as well as in jails and penitentiary death cells, for that matter, and among the damned. It isn't just education in itself which keeps a man from going down. If he is rotten inside, it may even speed him on his way.

What made her think that he was an educated man, in addition to his voice, was a Latin phrase which she thought she understood him to quote at one time. But she may have been mistaken about having heard it.

He hadn't thrust his conversation on them too much, anyway. He had settled back to enjoy the scenery, unobtrusively enough. He made no threat. He had accomplished his purpose in getting aboard that car with them. Now he effaced himself.

Still, he was there. She and Inis couldn't converse so freely between themselves. They must always be conscious of him. They must address a word back to him once or twice, moreover, because they knew that he was there. . . . She had asked him if the breeze was too much in back, because if so he might like to put up the rear windshield. And he had replied to her, no, that he liked the breeze. Inis had asked him what part of the country he came from, and if he got many rides. And he had replied that he came from nowhere in particular, and that he didn't get many rides, but that when he got one, he enjoyed it. She had asked him a little later if he was hungry. He had replied that he might do with a bite.

She told him that he might help himself to crackers and fruit, or whatever he could easily reach, and that when they stopped for supper he could have something more, if he was still with them—though perhaps by that time, she suggested, he would have wanted out. And he had replied that he enjoyed riding with them, and would keep on as long as they were going.

Inis had explained to him then that they were going to Vermont, driving all night. He had replied that he would like to go to Vermont, since he had never been there. He had offered to take the wheel to spell the young lady, if she got tired, later on. . . .

Just a word to him now and again that way, that had no significance, and a reply from him in his quiet voice, that had no particular significance, it seemed at the time, either. And in between times he was watching the scenery, there back of them, and eating a box of crackers that he had opened, and a banana that he had helped himself to.

They came over the crest of a hill, where the winding highway for the time was headed west; and in front of them, far beyond the blue Catskills, on the other side of the Hudson a hundred miles away, in that moment the red sun was going down.

Elinor slowed the car on the hill crest almost to a stop.

"There!" she said, with the tight feeling in her throat that sunsets had always given her all her life. "The sun is going down!"

She had forgotten in the moment the existence of that little mangy man back of her. She had forgotten even Inis, almost, at her side. A feeling of an intolerable desolation had hold of her, at sight of the red descending ball. It was something connected with the death of her young parents, killed in a theater fire when she had been little more than a baby, or with their interment at a sunset hour which she had witnessed. . . . The sun going down. The voice of the preacher and the weeping of the women, and all the west a fire.

"*Soles occidere et redire possunt*——"

She felt a strangling breath. *Suns may rise and sink again*—— She thought she heard the murmur of the words from the little man behind her. She turned her head around.

"*Nobis cum semel occidit brevis lux,*" she said, with tear-filled eyes.

But for us, when our brief light goes out——

And thought she heard the whisper of him finishing it, where he sat red-eyed behind her:

"*Nox est una perpetua dormienda.*"

There is one long night for sleeping!

How few men know their Latin any more!—Catullus's line to Lesbia.

One would not have expected her to understand it, with her young face, a word in a dead tongue. But not so long out of high school, and filled with books, she had. Those lines among her favorite.

But for that reason, of course, she may have merely imagined it. He may have been saying something else, actually. Or nothing at all. . . .

Whatever kind of voice he had, it was a voice to be noticed and remembered, it would seem. She remembered it. But that is all there is about his voice. There is no one except her who ever heard him. No one who is now alive.

He did not tell St. Erme and her that his name was Corkscrew, of course. He told them his name was Doc.

I have been looking over Rosenblatt's notebook again, his notes on Corkscrew.

There is the question of his height:

Q. [To Miss Darrie] You say that he was small, Miss Darrie. A small man. Do you mean that he was frail?

A. No, not frail. His torso and shoulders seemed normal in size, his arms rather long, with heavy wrists and hands. It was more that he was just sawed off. His legs seemed short for his body. He was only about five feet three inches tall.

Q. His legs seemed corkscrewed, his knees bent, as if he was crouching?

A. It was the baggy pants he wore, I think.

Q. If he had been crouching, and had straightened up, then he would have been a tall man?

A. No, not particularly tall. He could not have been so tall as Mr. Quelch here or Inis.

Q. About as tall as Dr. Riddle here, perhaps?

A. Yes, about that tall, he might have been, if he had been taller.

Q. That would be about five feet seven and a half.

A. [By Dr. Riddle] A good guess, Lieutenant. I am just five feet eight. . . .

There is the question of the color of his eyes, also, an important item in any system of police identification.

Q. [To Miss Darrie] His eyes were red, you say? You mean pink like an albino's?

A. No, the irises of his eyes were blue. A medium blue or gray. But his eyeballs, the whites of them, were inflamed and red, and even in the irises the red seemed to shine through. You noticed it at once.

Q. [To Dr. Riddle] What might that be?

A. It sounds as though it might have been chronic blepharitis.

Q. What's that, Doctor?

A. It's a condition of disease. However, I would not

care to make any positive statement without having seen him.

Q. You never saw him at all?

A. I have never seen him.

Q. If he knew something about medicine, there would be some things he could do to his eyes to make them look red, without having a disease, I suppose?

A. He would not necessarily have to know anything about medicine. . . .

There is also the matter of his torn ear, on which Rosenblatt seemed to place particular emphasis, since the ear is one of the most significant indices of identity according to the Bertillon system, as I understand it. And while the ordinary untrained observer does not pay attention to the shape of a man's ears, any great deviation from the normal in them no doubt would stand out.

The question comes up in the inquiry of Quelch, the somewhat garrulous postmaster at Whippleville, who was the last man to see that incredible killer before Dead Bridegroom's Pond.

Q. [To Mr. Quelch] You are the postmaster at Whippleville, Mr. Quelch? And you saw this man called Doc in the back seat of Mr. St. Erme's and Miss Darrie's car when they stopped at the post office in Whippleville about seven-thirty to inquire about some place where they might have a picnic supper?

A. Yes. I was standing on the front porch, just closing up, when this big gray car drove up, with that fellow in the back. It was going on seven-thirty-six, nearer than seven-thirty, and the afternoon mail from Pittsfield had been distributed, and nothing more till the mail truck at six o'clock tomorrow morning with the Danbury papers. There wasn't anybody left to talk to, so I thought I might as well go home and talk to the danged cat. Then this big car drove up. Miss Darrie was driving it, and a pretty picture she was, too, with her dark curly hair and her pink cheeks, and those blue-rimmed glasses she was wearing. And Mr. St. Erme said they were on their way to Vermont to get married, they were planning to drive all night, and they thought they would stop for a picnic supper; did I know any pretty places where they wouldn't be trespassing on anybody's front yard? And I said there was nothing but lakes and woods and rocks, nothing like Coney Island that they've got in New York, but some liked it, and they were welcome to it. And he said how about that road back there a couple of hundred feet, that road off to the side that they'd just passed, were there any pretty places on it? And I said that's the Stony Falls road and it's a bumpy, stony road and nobody lives on it but Old Man Hinterzee and John Wiggins that raises bees and has a cider mill, and two or three artists and old college professors that have their places they have bought to live at in the summers, but there are plenty of woods along it, and there's a lake up the road about a mile, about a mile this side of Old Man Hinterzee's, that doesn't belong to anybody, and it has woods and rocks around it, and he and his lady could have a picnic there, I guess, and it's a kind of pretty lake, only it's mighty black and deep, and some call it Lake Tagore, only most call it Dead Bridegroom's Pond. And Miss Darrie says to me, my goodness, what a dreadful name, why do they call it that? And I tell her that it's because a man named Bridegroom used to own it who's been dead a hundred years. And she says to him with a kind of little shiver that she doesn't like the sound of it, but he only laughs, and says what difference does it make. And he says thanks to me, they might try it, and after they have had their supper and are ready to go on, should they keep going up that road and find some other road off it to get them to Vermont, or should they come on back? And I said there's no road off it at all except the Swamp Road, about ten miles along, that all the swamp-rat Flails that is three-quarters Indian has always lived on, that twenty or thirty years ago used to raise so much hell, though there isn't any more of them left except John Flail now, with Two-finger Pete in the pen for murder and the rest of them all dead, and the Swamp Road didn't go nowhere, anyway, except to the old sawmill. And it was nineteen miles, or maybe twenty-one, to get on Route 49A at Stony Falls, and it's a bumpy stony road that's punishing on tires, and nobody ever takes it except the people that live on it, and them not too much; and him and his lady had better come back to Route 7 here and keep on it. And he says thanks again, they'll come back after they have had their picnic; and Miss Darrie here smiles at me, and they back and turn around, and go back down to the Stony Falls road a couple of hundred feet, and go on up it.

Q. You have given your conversation with Mr. St. Erme in great detail, Mr. Quelch, and I thank you for it. I am sure that you gave him complete directions. The question, however, is about this man who was with him and Miss Darrie—this tramp. You saw him in the back of the car, while they were stopped there at the post office?

A. Yes. I couldn't help but see him. They were stopped there, talking to me, about eight minutes and a half, more or less. I saw him setting in the back seat. I didn't look at him so closely, maybe. I was looking more at Miss Darrie setting at the wheel, she looked so young and pretty, she was pretty enough to be a pin-up girl, she was pretty enough to eat. More than him particularly. I didn't pay any particular attention to him, except that he must have been a hitchhiker they had picked up. I did notice he was wearing a coat with big black and white squares, and a light-blue hat with its brim cut saw-tooth all around, and he looked unshove and dirty; and his eyes were red and he had sharp pointed teeth. But I didn't notice how tall or short he was, setting down. He did have kind of long dry-looking reddish hair, come to think of it.

Q. What do you mean by red? Like Dr. Riddle's here?

A. Well, more auburn, maybe. More pinkish brown, with some gray in it, not so dark red quite.

Q. Could it have been a wig?

A. They make wigs better than that. I used to do some barbering over in Hartford, and I've seen some of these toupees and wigs they make so good I've snipped my shears to start to cut 'em, when a man sat down, before they took them off. This fellow's hair was awful rough cut, like he had done it in a mirror with a paring knife. No fellow would wear a wig like that.

Q. Did you notice his torn left ear, which Miss Darrie has described?

A. He was setting with his right side to me. He was kind of holding and pulling at his left ear, I think, now that you mention it. Maybe it was tore, but I didn't see it.

Q. Do you remember what his voice sounded like?

A. He didn't say anything. He just sat there in the back among the groceries.

Q. Have you seen him again since? I want you to think carefully before you answer me.

[Mr. Quelch, after deliberation, and after surveying a person present, states that he does not believe so.]

Q. [To Dr. Riddle] And you have not seen him since, either, Doctor?

A. I have never seen him at all.

He must have been real. He had an existence. Not merely she and St. Erme saw him, and Postmaster Quelch, but everyone else along the road from Dead Bridegroom's Pond as he raced in his crazy getaway.

There is old Hinterzee, gnarled and bow-legged, with his broken nose.

Q. [To Mr. Hinterzee] You were homeward-bound from the Whippleville post office up the Stony Falls road about a quarter of eight, and this gray car overtook you and passed you, Mr. Hinterzee, with Miss Darrie driving and Mr. St. Erme in front beside her, and this Doc, or Corkscrew, in the rear seat?

A. Yah.

Q. Miss Darrie has stated that she did not see anyone on the road.

A. I was down in ditch beside road. Tall grasses. I was looking for half dollar I lose last spring. Always when I go by, I stop and look for it. But I see them, yah. They go by.

Q. Describe this man we are referring to as Corkscrew.

A. He has black and white coat, funny cut blue hat, dirty face.

Q. A torn left ear?

A. I did not see. I was on right side of road.

Q. And you saw the car again, about ten or fifteen minutes later, and saw Miss Darrie and Mr. St. Erme and him, about half a mile farther along, where it had parked off the road beside the woods leading down to Dead Bridegroom's Pond? And Miss Darrie and Mr. St. Erme had got out of it and were going down through the woods toward the lake, and you saw Corkscrew slipping out of it and slipping down through the woods after them?

A. Yah.

Q. Describe how he was going after them, in your own words.

A. He was going creepy.

Q. Can you illustrate?

[Mr. Hinterzee crouches, makes a demonstration of a man stalking, lifting his feet carefully, parting bushes, with shoulders hunched.]

Q. Did he have a knife in his hand? A bread knife?

A. I did not see.

Q. What did you see?

A. They just going down through woods to lake, maybe have swim, maybe pick wild flowers. I see her white coat and his Panama down through trees. This fellow goes creeping after them. I go on.

Q. And you saw him again about forty minutes later, after you had reached your home, and were sitting on your front porch beside the road? He was driving the car, with Mr. St. Erme sitting slumped beside him with his head on the car door, one arm dangling overside, and Miss Darrie was no longer with them? And as he passed he howled his horn and laughed?

A. Yah.

Q. What did he laugh like?

A. Like a horse.

Q. Can you illustrate?

[Mr. Hinterzee puts his head sideways on his shoulder and utters a loud whinnying sound.]

A. Like that.

Q. What did you do?

A. I look at him. He is one crazy fellow.

Q. And Mr. St. Erme beside him did not move?

A. His arm moved. Swinging. Over the side of the door. His head on the car door maybe bounce, going over the bumps. The car goes by fast.

Q. [By Dr. Riddle] Excuse me, Lieutenant. His right arm, Mr. Hinterzee?

A. He was on the right side, yah. His right arm, it must have been.

Q. [By Dr. Riddle] And he had a hand at the end of it?

A. I did not see. But yah. He must have. If he did not have, I see. . . .

That is it. Hinterzee did not notice whether St. Erme had

a right hand. But if he had not had one, Hinterzee would have noticed. It is the abnormal item which sticks out. There was nothing abnormal about St. Erme in appearance. There was nothing wrong whatever with his right hand.

There he was. He lured them to stop and pick him up by the display of a dead mangled kitten, by some bird-charming power in his red eyes, by some hypnotic soothing quality in his soft quiet voice.

He got in and rode with them, looking at the scenery. He quoted Latin, and he pinched his ear.

When they stopped on the lonely road and went down to the lake shore, to examine it as a picnic site before bringing down their provisions, he followed them. For what? Merely to spy on them obscenely, out of a low-witted pleasure in watching people unaware, like the unknown man with the field glasses in the second-floor apartment across from her, at 511 West? To murder them down there now, and sink their bodies in the lake with stones?

St. Erme had acted like a man in a dream up to that moment, so far as concerned everything about Corkscrew. And even she, though uneasy over him at the beginning, seems for a while to have been half bewitched. They can't be blamed for that. Until he has been seen, it can't be understood. Some mesmerizing quality in him. Some power of suggestion.

Whatever his purpose with them was, he didn't have opportunity to attack them then and there. Down there by the black waters of the lake, in the twilight in the silent woods, with a horror impending. Suddenly, with death so near to her, she saw him peering down above her, and she screamed. And St. Erme awoke out of his hypnosis, out of his deadly dream.

Suddenly the spell was shattered by her scream. Suddenly St. Erme must have realized, however inadequately, that that negligible, contemptible, dirty, sawed-off little man was more than he seemed. Suddenly must have seen him as more than just a witless tramp—as a man with a keen and terrible brain behind his little red eyes. Suddenly must have been aware, however incoherently and incompletely, that this apparently harmless man whom he had let himself be lulled by, in his lordly condescension, was dangerous. Was the most dangerous man to him that he had ever met in the whole world.

But not enough. St. Erme didn't realize it quite enough. Not with a mortal dry-mouthed fear in him, for his own life, and for the girl's that he loved. Rather, he was enraged, with a lordly anger. Lordly, he pursued that red-eyed, cunning, dangerous little man. To rattle his bones, to beat the hell out of him, showing off his male courage, proud of his strength. And Corkscrew lured him back up toward the car, with the trick of the broken partridge wing.

The car keys are the answer to what he wanted, it can be hypothesized, in lack of any definite knowledge. St. Erme had taken charge of the keys again when he and Elinor had got out, as he had at the bank, and at their stops for lunch and in Danbury, with a pocket to slip them into. Corkscrew had seen him removing them, of course; but perhaps had not been sure whether he had pocketed them, or had dropped them for hiding in the grass beside the car.

Or perhaps it was the knife that he ran back to get. He flees back to the car, springs into it, and snatches up the knife. With it in hand, crouching on the seat, he turns, as St. Erme, hard after him, opens the car door to haul him out. With his red eyes, with his fanged grin, having now the advantage of height. And St. Erme, weaponless, lunges in to get him. With an angry bellow that turns to a scream.

He has the car keys now, Corkscrew. Out of St. Erme's pocket, if they were there. Or from the grass where St. Erme had dropped them—St. Erme having indicated by an involuntary glance of his eyes, at the demand, where they were hidden. He has St. Erme's money, too, those fifty crisp fifty-dollar bills which St. Erme drew at the bank this morning, that money which he may have carelessly displayed in Danbury, in the dark little ice-cream parlor or the grocery or the ten-cent store. He has everything. The thing is done.

But there is still the girl. He had better silence her, so she doesn't raise the alarm. He goes down swiftly after her where he last saw her. But she has left the lake. He comes back swiftly, calling her in a muffled, disguised voice, crudely attempting to imitate St. Erme's tones, using the names that he has heard St. Erme use to her.

"Elinor! Sweet!"

But at the same time swearing with an uncontrolled blasphemy, with a low flood of obscenities which St. Erme never knew. Not knowing that she is so near, that she can glimpse and hear him.

He finds her coat where she has abandoned it. She is hiding from him, she knows what he has done. Through the twilight woods he stalks her, silently, terribly, wasting no more breath.

Stalking her. With the knife. With his glaring eyes, beneath his saw-tooth hat, which seem—in a moment when they turn toward her, as he goes past—in the twilight now all ice and pale. And she lies hidden, with blood like ice. She creeps away. She lies hidden without a breath.

He can waste no more time with her. He must give it up. He goes back to the car, gets into it, and drives off, not pausing to dump St. Erme's body out, speeding up the road, away. . . .

An ordinary hitchhiker, thumbing by the roadside. A stolen car, and stolen luggage and money, with murder as an incident. A tedious, an ordinary story to the police. Every year, in almost every state.

But from the beginning Rosenblatt was not quite satisfied, I think. And I have a feeling, myself as well, that St. Erme's murder, and hers, also, were planned long ago.

There were she and St. Erme who saw him and heard him speak; there were Postmaster Quelch and old Hinterzee who saw him, more or less at length.

There was John Wiggins the beekeeper and his family, two miles on from Hinterzee's, who saw him—the Wigginses, whose big friendly St. Bernard dog he deliberately veered and struck, with malignant sadism, as it stood wagging its tail sluggishly beside the road, in sight of all of them, and then went speeding on, while Wiggins and his wife and their six children ran out and gathered the dying dog into their arms, with tear-blind eyes and breaking breasts, poor simple people, not knowing that there could be a fiend like him in all God's quiet simple world.

There was the refugee painter-musician-scene-designer Unistaire as well, half monkey and half faun, who was in his studio a mile and a half farther on, devising a surrealistic dance before his mirror to a composition of his own upon the phonograph, dressed in a leopard skin, a feather duster, and a chiffon nightgown, when Corkscrew drove that big gray car in off the road, and around the circular drive, fast and desperately—having mistaken Unistaire's drive for a side road, it would seem, and then realizing his mistake—with a squeal of tires and a scream of brakes, crashing down the wooden easel frames which Unistaire had set out on the drive with all his paintings on them—to impregnate them with the night dew, according to some theory of freshness in art he had—and back out onto the road again, and on up it, with a blare of wailing horn, as Unistaire went rushing out to see.

There was MacComerou himself, with his big old brain, working in his garden here three miles farther on, who saw him driving by red-eyed, with grinning pointed teeth, and recognized St. Erme as the man beside him who looked so white and ill. And though MacComerou hadn't seen enough to know that it was murder then, he had known that something wasn't right.

They all saw him. He was not invisible. After striking John Flail, he turned off down the Swamp Road. He abandoned the car at the end of the road, down beyond Flail's house. He had to pass me by to get there. There was no other way.

Q. [To Dr. Riddle] And you were at the Swamp Road entrance all during the murder hour, Dr. Riddle?

A. I was.

Q. And you didn't see the car pass you?

A. I didn't see it.

Q. And you didn't see this little sawed-off man we are speaking of as Corkscrew—this man with the red eyes, this man named Doc?

A. I did not see him. I have never seen him.

Q. And you are sure he didn't pass you?

A. Nothing passed me at all. . . .

I am back there. At that thing which has no answer. Why I didn't see him.

I must find the answer to that. Before the answer to why he did it. Even before the answer to where he is now. For without the answer to that, he will continue to remain invisible. Near as he is to me, and quiet as he is, now.

I must start from there. From where I was myself, at every moment during the hour of twilight last evening, which was the murder hour.

I had been driving down from John R. Buchanan's place in Vermont in this old coupe, on my way back to New York.

I had been summoned up there yesterday morning, Wednesday, suddenly, to operate on the old man for the brain malignancy of which he had been dying. It had been a big feather in my cap, maybe, that I should have been called in, instead of an older man. I had gone up with some hopes of performing some miracle.

But it had been a foredoomed failure; at his age, seventy-nine. He was already dying when I got there. His respiration and his pulse had stopped before I could begin my trepanation, on the table that had been set up for me. I looked at the white-starched anesthetist standing by, and pulled off my rubber gloves, and began to gather up my tools again.

"Don't take it so hard, Doctor," she said to me. "You look like a little boy whose pet kitten has been run over. There are always more cats."

She was one of these arch motherly souls. It was probably her stock phrase to all doctors in a like futile situation. I put my tools away.

I don't like corpses. I never have. To some people, I have

found, it seems an odd quirk in a doctor. But I always remember that Pasteur fainted more than once as a student
during dissections, and I respect him only the more for it.
One has to learn, and that is the only way. As a student
myself, I had stiffened my lip, and learned. But a doctor's
business is with life, with living tissue. When it ceases to be
alive, I'm through.

"Where are you going?" she said to me.

"Home," I said. "I'm through."

I had come up by special chartered plane, procured for
me by Buchanan's New York office. But there had been
no arrangements made to take me back. I asked Buchanan's housekeeper, or chatelaine, or whatever she was, about
trains; but there was none, she told me, till near midnight,
and this was only afternoon. She wanted to know how soon
I needed to be back in New York, and I told her not for
twenty-four hours necessarily, as I had made arrangements
to be away that long, but that I just wanted to get away now.
That I wished I had driven up.

She told me then that she had a car which she wanted to
get down to New York. It belonged to her boy, who was in
the air service. He had driven up in it to see her last month
before he went across, and had had to leave it, having re-
ceived his wire. Before coming up, he had made arrangements to sell the car to a New York dealer whose advertisement he had seen in the papers, and he wanted her to get it
down to the dealer to make his word good, and also to get
the money and have someone have the use of the car. It was

an old car, and she didn't know whether I would like to drive it down or not, but it would oblige her. She had enough gas saved up.

She was a fine woman, intelligent and understanding, as well as efficient, as she had to be, managing that big place and twenty servants. I don't know her name, although I was probably told it; unless it is on the card she gave me. Maybe she knew how badly I felt, and just wanted to help me get my mind off it, by giving me some small responsibility to carry out. Or maybe she really wanted to get the car down for her son. Or maybe both.

It was an old Draco coupe, when she showed it to me, in the garage with the dozen other cars, about ten years old, with battered fenders and torn upholstery, but its tires were good. I had had a Draco coach of that same vintage, which I had bought secondhand when I first started practice, before I got my Buick. It would be a lot pleasanter to get started back right away in it, I thought, instead of having to wait around at the house here, or at the station, for the train, and perhaps stand in a crowded coach for a good part of the night. The drive down on the main highways would be through pretty scenery all the way, and the driving alone would help to take my mind off it. I ought to make New York by midnight, or maybe even ten o'clock.

"Here's the dealer's card with his name on it," she told me. "Tell him I'll mail him the bill of sale when he has sent his check. And here's your own fee or honorarium, do you call it, Doctor?"

"Wage," I said. "When I earn it. If I'd earned it, I would send a bill. I can't take anything."

"Mr. Buchanan always liked to pay his obligations promptly," she told me. "It was one of the last instructions that he gave, about you. He knew that you would do your best, if anything could be done. If nothing could be done, you had still earned it. Please take it. If you won't, I would feel—dreadful."

The old man's death had cut her up, of course. With me, it was a professional failure. But with her, it was the severing of a relationship.

"I have been with him twenty years," she said. "He would not want to see his last bill unpaid."

"Thanks," I said. "In that consideration, I'll take it."

She gave me the card of the dealer to whom I was to deliver the car, and an envelope that had some bills in it. The old man, it seemed, had been one of those who like to pay in cash, not by check. I stuck them into my pocket, without looking at either of them. When I got down to the city I could see who the dealer was, and phone him to pick up the car at 511 West, or take it around myself tomorrow morning, if his place wasn't too far away. I didn't want to look at the money at all until I got it to my bank, the Lexington Trust on Forty-seventh, and deposited it with young Sawyer, the teller I generally did business with there. I didn't even want to think of it.

So that was how I happened to be driving down. I stowed

my surgical case and the overnight bag I had brought along in the trunk compartment, and started out.

The anesthetist, I think, would have liked to have come along with me. She hinted at it. I wonder, if she had, whether she would be dead now, too.

It was just about sunset when I turned off onto this side road, to get over from Route 49A to Route 7 as a short cut on my map.

I had not entirely shaken off my sense of depression over my failure, it may be. However, I cannot assume that it was in any subconscious mood of flight that I turned off. It looked shorter on the map, and I wanted to save time and gas.

The place where I turned off was called Stony Falls. It was just a little general store and a few houses. The road ran over to Route 7 at a place called Whippleville. It cut off about fifteen miles. But it was a terribly narrow, winding, up-and-down stony road, I found when I got on it, and I had to slow down and drive carefully to save the tires.

I kept on, hoping it would get better soon. But it didn't. It was practically an abandoned road. There were only two or three dilapidated farmhouses that I passed in the next nine or ten miles, and none of them appeared occupied. On both sides the road was lined with old stone fences, overgrown with great ropy vines of poison ivy with glistening warty leaves that must have been a hundred years old. Beyond the fences there were only woods, deserted fields, boulder-strewn hillsides, and more woods. It was the kind of road one drives along in a nightmare. I had been going along it about half an hour when the engine stalled.

It just choked and died. The car rolled on a few yards more, and stopped. About a half-hour after sunset. I didn't look at my watch, but there was red still in the sky.

The place where I had stopped was right at the junction of a dim side road going off to the left. A half-rotted sign-post with three arms stood there beside the road. There were old hand-molded lead letters on the arms, and lead pointers shaped like hands, which might have dated back to Revolutionary days. One of them pointed back the way I had come, saying "Stony Fa 9 M"; and one pointed down the road ahead, saying "Whipl'vl' 10 M"; and one pointed off down the road beside me, saying "Swamp Rd. 15/8 M to Flail's Saw Mill."

It was only the shadow of an old wagon road, its deep ruts overgrown with purple asters and yellow daisies and other weeds. It didn't look as if a wheel had passed over it for the past forty years. It was the first side road of any kind, though, that there had been since I left Stony Falls. It went along for about two hundred yards in sight, and then was lost in deep hemlock woods.

I saw the figure of a man walking away from me near where the road vanished in the woods, in that moment as I came to a stop. He was a black-haired man, without a hat, wearing khaki pants and a blue denim shirt that was dark with sweat over his shoulder blades, and was carrying his coat slung over his shoulder. He seemed to be a powerfully built man, above medium height, and he was walking with a soft shambling stride, flat-footedly, like an Indian.

He didn't turn around when I began grinding the starter. He merely went shambling on, down the weedy road two hundred yards away from me, and in a moment had vanished among the trees. . . .

It is possible, I acknowledge, that he did not exist. That he was only a hallucination. Hallucinations are not impossible with anyone, given a certain light and a certain absent state of mind. And though I am not imaginative, it is possible that he existed only in my mind, shambling along the weedy road there away from me, with his coat thrown over his sweat-stained back, and vanishing into the dark woods.

The problem is not of the phantasm of a man I saw who did not exist, however. The problem is of a murder car I did not see, which did.

I stepped on the starter, and the engine caught. But before I could let in the clutch, it died again. It caught again when I stepped on it again. And died.

It was one of those teasing and exasperating things, where every moment you think you almost have it, and so keep on. I had half a tank of gas still, so it couldn't be that. I tried the choke. I tried it with switch on, and off. I wore down the battery, starting it that way, and then having it stall on me. When it wouldn't turn over any more, I got out and cranked.

I may be obstinate, but I don't like to be licked. I would

cut the switch, and swing the crank over half a dozen times to suck a charge in, and then go back to the instrument board and turn the switch on, and back to the crank and snap it over, hard. Each time the engine would catch, and then after a couple of kicks would choke and die away; and I would have to do the same damned thing all over. By the tenth or fifteenth try I had grown a little tired or careless, and didn't have the crank engaged properly when I gave it the starting snap. It flew out and went whirling past my head. If I hadn't ducked, it would have brained me. It nicked the lobe of my left ear, drawing a little blood, as it was. But the cartilage didn't seem torn, when I felt it.

I must have tried it twenty times or more, getting more sweaty and dirty and red-eyed. I'm not a truck driver in build, a hundred and forty pounds, but my arms are plenty wiry, and I have strong hands, as a surgeon must. Still I got played out at last, with a ripping headache down my skull.

The evening was so hot and still. Even after the last sunset glow had disappeared and the twilight shadows were gathering over everything, the stones of the road still gave forth their stored-up heat. If it had been midday I might have got a sunstroke, and in that case conceivably could have drawn a blank for a few minutes without knowing it. But the sun had gone down. A mild heat prostration was what I had, with a bad headache, but not any blackout.

I remember thinking in the back of my mind that I ought to push the car off the middle of the road, if anybody should come along, because I was blocking it. But I didn't bother to do it, because nobody came along.

Once, while I was cranking, I did think I heard the wail of a far-off horn behind me, and the hum of a car coming up the road. I straightened up and looked around, wiping the sweat from my face. But nothing came up the road. The eerie wail might have been only a railroad train off in some valley, and the humming some airplane over the hills and out of sight.

A kind of whirling little heat gust came spinning up the road while I stood there, looking. It brushed against me as it passed, and went brushing on. I could watch how it went, though I couldn't see it. It veered away, after brushing me, and went off down the Swamp Road, bending the weeds and grasses and turning the undersides of them to silver, and skirling up a little sandy dust in the ruts like the smoke of a car going fast. But it wasn't a car. Not anything visible. It was just a little whirl of air in motion.

It was while I was following it with my gaze that I saw the yellow rattlesnake. It was lying in one of the ruts of the Swamp Road about twenty feet away from me, staring at me with motionless eyes in its flat head.

A timber rattler, about four feet long, the color of dead grass, with pale milk-chocolate markings—a female, if it's true, as is sometimes said, that the lighter-colored ones are females. I don't know how long it had been there when I saw it. But the probability would be that it had been there all the time, or I would have seen it crawling. A moving snake catches the eye; and this one was lying yellow and still, mingled with the yellow roots of the wheel-rut grasses.

There was nothing strange in a rattler lying there on the old dead road. There are plenty of them in the hills all the time, and particularly out on old roads in August. They like to lie in the heat of the sun-baked dust and stones, to shed their skins. They are apt to be more or less blind at that time, and anything that comes along may run them over. The only thing at all unusual about this particular yellow snake that I noticed was the color of its eyes. Most rattlers have mottled golden eyes. But this one's were red as fire. That may have been due to some last shred of infrared sunset still lingering in the sky, beyond the range of my spectrum, but not of its, and reflecting on its hard, lidless eyes with that burning color.

I wasn't sure but that it was dead. It might have been run over. But I jerked out the crank handle and hurled it at it, anyway. The iron hit the stony ruts with a whirling thud, right where that broad motionless fanged head had been. But there was nothing there now. It had not been dead or blind. All the time lying there, maybe hours, maybe days, but still whip-quick at the flash of danger. At my gesture it had slid instantly, and was gone.

That figure of a man vanishing down the road, and the whirling little gust that came up behind me and turned off and went brushing down the road, and the yellow rattlesnake lying in the ruts, were the only things I saw during the time I was stalled there at the entrance to the Swamp Road.

I didn't clock the time, but I was there from a little after sunset till twilight was falling, a period of a good hour, at least. I was nearly ten miles away from Dead Bridegroom's Pond.

The crank had bounced off into the tall grass at the edge of the old road. I didn't bother to go and retrieve it for the moment. It wouldn't do me any good if I kept cranking all night, unless I located what the trouble was. I lifted up the hood, to see if I could diagnose it.

I'm not an expert mechanic, by any means. But a car's internal machinery is like a man's, in one way, which is that there are just so many different organs, and just so many ways in which they can go wrong. I had to study the engine, trying to figure what each thing was for, where a garage repairman would have known at sight, and how it was all put together. Maybe if a garage repairman should try to do an anatomical section for the first time, he would be just as stumped, and have to figure it out. Still, if he had any brains at all he ought to be able to see how the joints and tissues were put together, in a fashion, after a while, by using his commen sense; and I should hate to think that I wasn't as bright, at his trade.

It must be some dirt that had got into the intake feed line of the vacuum. That was the only thing which could make it keep choking off that way. It couldn't be anything else. I remembered I had had the same trouble once with my old Draco coach, with an engine like this; only, on that occasion there had been a mechanic handy to diagnose the difficulty and straighten it out for me before I had cranked myself dizzy.

It wasn't a very complicated operation, as I recalled it. All I needed to do was unscrew a little hexagonal nut and disconnect the line, clean out a little filter screen, suck out the dirt from the line with my mouth till the gas flowed clear, and then tighten the nut up again. The thing oughtn't to take more than five minutes with a small wrench. I should have tried to find the trouble in the first place, instead of wasting all that time. I'd have saved myself a ripping headache, if I had, and been halfway down to Danbury by now.

I rummaged around for tools under the car seat, but all I could find was a jack without a handle, a lug wrench for changing tires, and a bunch of rusty chains. It was damned silly. All I needed was almost any kind of small wrench, or even a pair of ordinary pliers; but I couldn't do it with my fingers or my teeth. I looked in the trunk compartment in the back, but there weren't any tools there, only my bag and my kit of instruments. And there was nothing in the latter which would be of any use for that kind of job. I closed the lid down again.

There hadn't been any house that had looked occupied, where I might borrow a wrench, since I had turned off at Stony Falls. That shambling figure which had vanished down the Swamp Road, and the rutted way itself, didn't look very promising. I decided to go on down the road ahead to see if I could find a house.

I left my coat on the car seat, and the keys in the ignition lock. It didn't seem likely that anyone would come along that God-forsaken road while I was away.

Still, I did take the envelope from my coat pocket that Mrs. X, old John R. Buchanan's chatelaine, had given me, and folded it and stuck it into my hip pocket. It felt rather thick and waddy. There might be as many as fifty bills in it, I thought. I wondered if the old man had told her to give me fifty dollars, all in ones. That would be rather mean. More likely it was fifty tens, five hundred dollars, which would be a fair price for doing nothing.

There were cicadas singing in the twilight as I went along. The road was still narrow and stony. It was bordered by deep ditches on either side, filled with dusty, waist-high weeds; and beyond them the eternal poisonivy stone fences without a break. On the other side of the fences were woods of oak and pine, and now and then a clump of silver birches. In a hundred feet I had rounded a bend and lost sight of the car back at the fork.

I had gone about a quarter mile when I saw an old shin-gled farmhouse at my right, a hundred feet off the road among tall weeds and a furze of second-growth. I slowed when I came abreast of it, looking it over. But the windows were eyeless, and the chimney bricks were fallen in a heap of rubble at one end of it, while the roof was only a skeleton of ridgepole and naked rafters in the silver air. Even the gap in the stone fence where the entrance gate had been was filled with thick high weeds, and the road that had gone in could no longer be made out.

I had veered a couple of feet off the high crown of the road, before seeing that the place was abandoned. My foot struck something soft as I started on. I stopped again to look down at it. It was a dirty shapeless old blue felt hat, lying on the road.

It certainly was the damnedest-looking hat. Its brim had been cut away in saw-tooth scallops all around, and crescent and star-shaped holes had been cut in its crown, in the way boys and boy-witted men sometimes do to old hats. It was just lying there, with no one around that it might belong to, while in the woods and weedy fields on either side insects creaked and sang.

I don't know what impelled me to stoop and pick it up. Perhaps because of its color. It was filthy with ingrained dirt and grease. But it was—or it had been once—of a soft lovat-blue color. I have always been partial to lovat-blue hats, though they're not always easily obtainable in the hat shops. I had bought the last one I had owned during my final year in medical school, and had worn it four or five years, and might have been wearing it yet if my secretary hadn't screamed. I still had it, the same way most men keep their old hats, on a shelf of my closet back at 511 West.

This cut-up hat had the texture of what had once been

a good piece of felt, in spite of its dirt, when I picked it up. And no wonder, since it had the colophon of Haxler's on Fifth Avenue, where I bought my own hats. I pulled down the sweatband—a 7⅜. Looking more closely, I could see where paper initials had been pasted on the band. They had peeled off; but the stained and darkened leather was still a little lighter where they had been, and I could make their shape out: "H.N.R., Jr."

It was my own old hat. No one's else. Here on this road, all chopped up that way. When had I last seen it on my closet shelf? Last week, or last winter? I would have said only yesterday. A man puts something away, and thinks of it as being just where he put it. Its image is in his mind. Yet it might have been a good many months since I had last actually seen that old hat on my shelf. Maybe as far back as last fall Mrs. Millens had given it to the janitor or the Salvation Army, in a fit of ridding up, as she calls it, without bothering to tell me.

It gave me a queer feeling of a lost kinship. I couldn't help but have it. To find it lying here on the deserted road, a hundred miles from home, filthy and mutilated, but still something that had once been an integral part of my appearance and personality. A hat is more intimate than a necktie or even than a pair of gloves. It is a kind of badge of a man's individuality, of his profession and his rank. The king's crown, and the peasant's mobcap; banker's Homburg or cowboy's sombrero, a headpiece and the way a man wears it show his character and set his style. This had been my hat, and I had always worn it a little at an angle.

Now it was cut with a knife into the shape of a clown's hat. I wondered what kind of man had last worn it. If he had liked the color, too.

I had probably got fifty different species of bacteria and protozoa on my finger tips just in the brief handling I had given it. I tossed it over into the deep weeds beside the road.

There was a crushed grasshopper lying on the road, which had been under the hat when I picked it up. I took the insect up between my thumb and forefinger. A gray stony dust was ground into its body, from a car tire or a heel that had trodden on it. It had been crushed at some time before the hat had dropped.

Its feelers were still stirring, and brown saliva was oozing from its mandibles. Its front legs were crossed as if in prayer. Its black eyes were as black as blank black shining quartz or glass. They were still alive, to some degree, I suppose, but I don't think they were aware of me.

I don't know how long crushed insects take to die. But probably not very long. The hat had been here even less a time than that. Perhaps the boy or man who had dropped it would discover his loss, and come back soon looking for it, if he was fond of it. I might as well have left it where I had found it on the road.

I crushed the insect's thorax in my fingers, and tossed it, too, into the ditch.

The eyeless old house with its skeleton roof stared at me across the high weeds in the silver twilight, and cheepers throbbed, and cicadas shrilled. I heard a croaking in the ditch, like a bull-throated frog, as I arose.

"Awrg!"

And then again, "Awrg!"

Slow, with long seconds in between, as if pausing for a tremendous breath. A sound that was quite inhuman.

There was a faint stirring in the dusty weeds as I went on, though no more than a frog might make. I went on down the road. There had been no reason I should stop for an inhumanly croaking frog. . . . Yet if my headache had not been with me still, doubtless I should have recognized it as significant that, subconsciously, I had thought of that slow croak as inhuman. One does not think of a frog's croak as inhuman. It is the croak of a frog. One only thinks of something as inhuman which should be human.

And perhaps is, in part.

A half mile or three quarters farther on I began to come at last to the indications of inhabited civilization— the first I had seen since I had turned off at sunset on this nightmare way, the first sign of any human life even—and I began to breathe more normally, as if some tense scene in a play, or some exhausting and frightful work I had been doing, was over.

The unbroken warty ivy-grown stone fence had given way on both sides of me—on my left to a bushy twelve-foot hedge of California privet, thick with white sweet-smelling blossoms that in the daytime must be a treat for bees, and on my right to a whitewashed snake fence, bordering a gnarled old apple orchard in tall grass. The road surface seemed to be growing a little better, too—still stony, but not so much, and a little wider and more level, as if it might have been graded at some time in the past forty years.

There was a red composition roof above the hedge in a moment more, and a glimpse of a newly painted white gable. A telephone line came up this far, I saw, along the road in front of me, with a wire from the last pole going in across the hedge to the house.

That tenuous, slight wire, looping in across the hedge, was like a life line. After that long lonely road of eyeless houses, of poison fences and woods and weedy fields, of a phantasmal figure vanishing, of the singing of the insects in the empty twilight and of that old mutilated hat of mine, and all the other damned lonesomeness of it, it was like suddenly emerging into the living world of sane and ordinary things again.

I had drawn no blank, certainly. I had suffered no cataleptic trance. I had been conscious every minute of the past hour since I had turned off onto this road at sunset. Perhaps even hyperconscious. But I had just been so damned alone. The feeling of being stuck, of being maybe ten times farther than I had actually been from anywhere—as it was turning out—and of having, perhaps, to spend the night ahead in walking, had magnified and intensified every minute. But my situation hadn't really been so bad as I had thought. And now it wasn't bad at all any longer.

To a civilized man, beyond the simple animal need for food, the greatest necessity is a contact with other men, I decided. The dregs of the headache were still in me, but my skull was no longer split in two. However remote in miles from the nearest city I might still be now, or even from the next house, a phone line was a contact with the whole world, and with everything in it. With restaurants, taxis, laundries, garages, hospitals, or the police. With the news of the hour and the talk of men, as instantly as if the whole world were only beyond a wall, in an adjacent room.

I was hungry, but a phone could get me food, or get me a car that would take me to it. I was filthy, but from somewhere, at some price, I could get clean clothes. If I couldn't get the car started by my own efforts now, where I had left it stalled back there by the dead sign at the entrance to that phantasmal rutted road, I could get a garage man from the next town to do it for me, or from some town, even if I had to offer him a hundred dollars to come down from Pittsfield or up from Danbury. . . .

A man has to go along a nightmare road with a splitting skull, to appreciate all the meaning of a phone.

A hundred feet along the privet hedge I came to the entrance of a graveled, suburban-looking driveway, with tire tracks on it.

The red-roofed cottage was only fifty feet inside—a story-and-a-half Berkshire colonial, painted white with red shutters, with a mass of Paul's Scarlets covering one side. A lawn of white clover and long blue grass was in front of it, and there was a flower garden in the back.

Beyond the house, another hundred and fifty feet or so, up at the end of the drive, there was a substantial-looking barn, big and modern, painted white and with a red roof, also, and with a cupola rising from the center of its roof ridge, topped by a spire with a brass grasshopper weather vane. Like the famous grasshopper vane on Faneuil Hall, I think, in Boston.

A station wagon with a flat tire stood out on the drive in front of the barn, headed toward the doors, but not yet put away. There was a whitewashed pigpen and some chicken-houses to one side, though no pigs or chickens in them. Back beyond the barn was a windmill and a water tank, up on a little rise of ground, and rock-studded pastures and copses of evergreens, back to a line of woods.

It was the kind of pretty little country place with some city comforts, *urbs in rure*, which somebody had spent some moderate money, thought, and pleasure in fixing up. The house, with its old fanlight and tiny attic windows, must be an old eighteenth-century original, restored to its simple pristine lines from whatever gingerbread decorations had been added by intervening fancy-loving generations. It was the summer home of some cultivated man, I knew it, of simple tastes, with a fondness for solitude and old things—for reading books, and perhaps writing them, and puttering in his garden. Perhaps a retired college professor, I thought; and—because of the Faneuil weather vane—probably from Boston.

There was a mailbox stuck on a five-foot pole at the edge of the road, beside the drive. "A. MacComerou," it said simply, in small stenciled letters.

The name, somewhat unique, rang a bell in my mind. It couldn't be the name of anyone in the medical profession, for medical doctors are always particular about advertising their degrees. Almost any of us would sooner appear without a shirt than without his Dr. or M.D., particularly on his mailbox. I was reminded of medical school, all the same. Then it clicked. *Homicidal Psychopathology*, by Adam MacComerou, which had been our textbook in Med Psych 12 during my senior year.

There was never another textbook like it. I could still feel the weight of it, just lifting it, and see again before my eyes its somber brown buckram binding, enclosing its twelve hundred and eighty-seven pages of fact-packed small-type text, with notes and indices. *Selected Case Histories in an Approach to an Examination of the Basic Problems of Homicidal Psychopathology, Together with a Brief Inquiry into Certain Aspects of Aberrant and Divided Personality Among Men of Superior Mentality, by Adam MacComerou, A.B., Ph.D., Litt.D. (causa honoris, Chicago), Sc.D. (Yale), LL.D. (Swarthmore, Colum-bia, McGill), Lowell Professor of Psychiatry at Harvard,* was the full title page of it, as I remembered it. *Hom. Psych.* was what we had always called it, for short.

Old Adam knew his murderers. The dull and ponderous title had been deliberately fabricated, he had explained in one of his dry footnotes, to keep screwball laymen away, who might have found themselves too much interested in it, oth-erwise. He knew the power of suggestion on weak minds. Actually *Hom. Psych.* had been anything but dull and heavy. Lucidly written, wise, and full of meat, it was more dramatic than most fiction, in the stories it told of murderous mental-ities and its analyses of just what had made them like that. As a textbook, of course, it would always be a classic in its field, the final word.

This A. MacComerou couldn't be old Adam himself, of course. He must be dead by now, with all that had been in his brain. It mightn't even be any relation, or anyone who had ever heard of him. Still, it wasn't a very usual name.

I felt a momentary hesitation, I recall it. I had been fas-cinated by *Hom. Psych.* when I had had it, at an impres-sionable age. I had memorized whole paragraphs of it, and had passed it with an A. MacComerou, I had always felt, was a great mind.

Yet I wasn't sure whether I should care to meet him now, in person, if it was the same.

I must get that item analyzed in my mind—my feeling

in that moment as I stood there beside the mailbox, before going in, at twilight. My feeling that I would rather it didn't turn out to be old Adam MacComerou himself.

In part, of course, I was tired, and had a headache—I didn't particularly want to meet any man too intelligent, who might want to converse too much. In part, I think it was due to a general feeling I have that authors and their books are separate things; and that if a man has written a great book, the best of him is in it. An author and his book are no more identical than a father and his child, or a man and his wife. They are related, and they have a similarity in various ways; but you can like one without liking the other. They are not the same.

But it was something more than that. Old MacComerou had found a particular quiet amusement in poking fun at medical doctors in various paragraphs all through *Hom. Psych.*, in a quiet and good-humored way, but at the same time also somewhat irritating. The medical profession hadn't been very advanced in its understanding of the problems of mental disorders at the time he had written it; and some of the more ignorant medical doctors had even branded psychiatry as a quack science. It was like astrology or phrenology, they had said, pseudoscientific bait for fools.

Old Adam had been too great a man to enter into any exchange of name calling. But he had naturally found some amusement in pricking, in his quiet way, at practitioners of medicine and surgery, here and there, in his book. He wouldn't have been human if he hadn't. One of the most interesting chapters in *Hom. Psych.* was the one called "Jekyll-Hyde, M.D.," in which he had gathered together the case histories of murderers who had all happened to be doctors. I'll admit that he had plenty there.

But it didn't mean that, just because I was a doctor, he would find a murderer in me, of course. . . .

There was a gray bird with a white breast, a phoebe, that fussed and flew low before my eyes in that moment as I paused at the entrance to the drive. She had built her nest in a cylinder-shaped newspaper box, open at both ends, that was close beside the mailbox, I saw, and there were nestlings in it. Phoebes generally have several broods that way, all summer, and are devoted parents. Generally, too, they are friendly birds, nesting around houses as they always do, and being accustomed to humans.

But this particular mother Phoebe might never have seen a man before, from the way she reacted to me. Flying back and forth across my face on gray wings in the twilight, as if I were some kind of bloody panther she would beat back with her white breast, with her soft twittering cries.

I heard a tinkling sound beyond the hedge as I started in, and a feline wail. A gray cat with white paws and a white face, wearing a collar jangling with little bells, came slinking out from the roots of the hedge onto the gravel, almost at my feet. It looked up at me with a hoarse twanging wail coming from its throat, like the wail of a steel guitar.

It wasn't a homeless hunting cat. It was a tame cat, a

house cat, with its bell-studded collar. It lived here, since pet cats stay around the places they belong. And I usually get along with cats. They come to rub against me without much urging. Even those in the experimental laboratory which I used to take care of when I was a student, poor things. I have always thought I had a way with cats. I stooped and held out my hand to this one now, with a soothing word. But it only looked at me with its yellow eyes, miaowing, and veered away. It went loping up the drive away from me with its head and tail down, leaping into the tall grass a little farther on, with its hoarse and wailing cry.

There was that mangled gray kitten which Corkscrew had in his arm, and dropped in the ditch beside the highway when Elinor and St. Erme had stopped to see. But there is no way it can be tied up with the wailing of that gray cat of MacComerou's at sight of me. No way whatever.

No lights had been lit in the house yet. I could hear a woman's voice talking some place inside, though, through the closed windows, and then another's voice replying, as I went up the drive; so somebody, anyway, was home.

There was a slow, regular, whacking sound, like someone beating a heavy carpet, out in back. Country houses are usually entered from the kitchen way, and I went back there, following the sound.

Behind the house was the garden I had glimpsed, with swarms of rosebushes heavy with pale full-blown blossoms—cream or yellow, I could not be sure in the silver light, but making a heavy fragrance in the air. Tall delphinium spikes and hollyhocks, and clusters of little pale summer chrysanthemums, grew in beds around, and the air was sweet with all their smells, and the damp smell of grass and good black garden earth.

There were little stone paths between the flowers, and a mirror ball like a clairvoyant's crystal ball stood on a white wooden pedestal in the middle of a grass plot, to catch and reflect all the colors of the flowers. They were all subdued now, and the ball was as silver as the twilight sky.

A tall, sinewy, bent-shouldered man in a pair of striped shorts and moccasins was packing down the earth with the flat of a spade in the bed across from me, with his back turned to me. He had a bald head rimmed by a thin fringe of clipped whitish hair, big bat ears, and compressed and toothless jaws.

He paused in his whacking as I stepped on the garden path, gripping the spade handle with one brown hand, and waving his other hand around his neck and shoulders, with a long thin white arm like a wavering white snake.

"Get away, you damned bloody little fiend!" he said, in a mushy voice.

He wasn't talking to me. He hadn't heard me walking up the broad shallow tire tracks in the driveway gravel, in my prewar crepe-soled sport shoes. He didn't know that anyone was within three miles of him, perhaps. Just slapping at mosquitoes, and talking to himself, as a man gets to do alone.

"Damn you, you red bloody——"

Whack!

"Excuse me," I said, pausing by the mirror ball, with a hand on it.

He had squashed a bloated mosquito on top of his bald skull. It made a smear on his palm as he lifted it. He stood there with his face to the flower bed he had been working at, holding his hand motionless two inches above his head.

"Yes?" he said, in a whisper.

"I was wondering——" I said, a little hesitantly.

"Yes?" he repeated.

As if he were concentrating, not quite sure whether he had heard my voice, or had only imagined it. And if he had heard it, and not just imagined it, where in hell it had come from—whether it had come from inside the house, where the subdued voices of those two women were still talking and gabbling, or whether it had come from the general dusk around him, or maybe from the ground.

"Here I am," I said. "Behind you."

"Behind me," he repeated.

He turned around, with his shoulders bent, gripping his spade with both brown hands. There was a gray furze on his pale chest. His face was sunbrowned, like his hands, darker than his arms and body, and he had brown outstanding ears, like a huge bat. He stared at me with compressed and toothless jaws, with pale-blue searching eyes, across the silver dusk.

"Where in hell did *you* come from?" he said, with his toothless jaws, after a moment. "Who are you?"

I took my hand from the mirror ball. I walked toward him.

"My name's Riddle," I said. "Dr. Harry Riddle, of New York. My car is stalled up the road. I wondered if you knew of a garage man around——"

"A garage man?" he mumbled, staring at me.

"I didn't really expect to find one," I said. "I think I might be able to take care of the trouble myself, if I had a small wrench. All I need is just to unscrew a nut. I haven't any tools in my car. Any kind of small adjustable wrench, or a pair of pliers, ought to do the trick, if you have any."

His mouth spread in a friendly grin, with a twinkle of humor wrinkling about his shrewd old gaze.

"You have a damned light, quiet way of walking, for a redheaded man," he said toothlessly. "You gave me a small wrench yourself. Turn-about is fair play. You want to unscrew a nut, do you? Well, I imagine that we ought to be able to find something around the place here for that purpose. What is your name again—Riddle? Dr. Riddle. My name is Professor Adam MacComerou, Dr. Riddle. I guess you saw it on the mailbox."

He shifted his spade to his left hand, extending his right to me. His palm was cool, smooth, and strong.

"Are you *the* Adam MacComerou?" I asked him.

"The?" he said, looking at me a little warily, as if wondering what problem of screwball murder I was going to spring on him if he admitted that he was. "I am Professor Mac-Comerou, yes. I don't suppose there are so many."

"I had you in Med Psych 12 my senior year," I said.

"Harvard?" he asked me. "You took some course——"

I could see from the way he looked at me that he knew he didn't know me, and yet on the other hand had a feeling that he ought to, for some reason.

"No," I said. "Southern State. I wasn't one of your students. You've never seen me, Professor. We used your book, I meant. It was almost our Bible."

"Oh," he said. "Well, there's a lot of interesting stuff in it. I suppose a good many have read it."

He gave a final whack to the ground with the flat of his spade, and tossed it over on the edge of a flower bed, toward the kitchen porch.

"Are you a gardening nut yourself, Doctor?" he asked. "I was just setting in my next spring's tulips," he told me, when I shook my head. "A garden takes a lot of time. There's always something. . . . Your car's stalled up the road, you say? I don't know of any garage mechanic around. But we'll see what we can do to get you going. Where is your car located? You must be this side of Unistaire's, or you'd have stopped in at his place. You're heading up towards Stony Falls?"

"No," I said. "I'm coming down from Stony Falls. I'm heading towards Whippleville to get over on Route 7. My car's up in that direction."

"Oh," he said. "You came from that direction?"

"Yes," I said. "From that direction. I'm heading over from 49A. I turned off at Stony Falls."

"I see," he said. "You must have had quite a walk. No one living anywhere along the road from here to Stony Falls."

He seemed to be waiting for me to say something, but I didn't know what he wanted me to say.

"I suppose you saw that gray car with the two men in it going by you?" he said.

"No," I said. "I didn't see anything go by."

I don't think he was thinking too much about the car he had asked me about, at the moment. There was something about me that bothered him. Something he found missing, I should say.

"They must have got out at Stony Falls onto 49A before you turned off there," he said. "It may have been as much as a half-hour ago that they went by."

"I turned off onto the road here at Stony Falls at sunset," I said. "An hour or an hour and a half ago. I've been on it ever since. There wasn't anything that went by."

"At sunset?" he said, with a frown. "You've been on the road an hour and a half? Are you sure? And you didn't see a gray Cadillac phaeton with its top down, with red cushions? A New York license number XL four hundred thousand something? With a little red-eyed hairy-faced man in a blue saw-tooth hat and a checked coat at the wheel, and a black-haired, black-eyed young fellow in a gabardine suit sitting in a rather sprawled, stiff position beside him?"

"No," I said. "I didn't see it. It didn't go by me."

"It must have turned off the road just before it reached you," he said. "It worried me a little when I saw it. That fellow at the wheel was such an ugly little devil. He had pointed cat teeth, and a torn ear. What happened to your own ear, by the way?"

"My crank flew off while I was cranking——"

But he wasn't interested. He was revolving some problem in his mind. I followed him to the back porch.

"The black-haired young fellow with him looked like that young fellow what's-his-name," MacComerou said, mumbling over his shoulder to me. "Young St. Erme, I think his name is, the young oil millionaire from Oklahoma. A fine, likable type of young business executive. I couldn't understand what he would have been doing in company with a man like that."

It was the first time I had ever heard St. Erme's name. The very first.

"I've never heard of him," I said.

"No, I suppose not," said MacComerou. "He hasn't been in New York very long, as I understand it. A. M. Dexter, of the Dexter Day and Night Garage on West Fourteenth Street, introduced him to me one time when I was having my car serviced. St. Erme is a kind of silent partner of Dexter's, I understand, in developing some highly secret war devices.

"That's one thing that worried me about it," he added. "For another, St. Erme is the sort of young fellow who always likes to carry a lot of money. He was sitting beside that tramp with his head on the back of the seat, looking up at the sky. His face was like wax. His lips seemed moving, and I assumed he was saying something to the laughing little fiend at the wheel. But it might have been some prayer he was uttering, when I think it over. Or only the wind on his face."

"They didn't pass by me, I'm sure of it," I said.

"They must have turned off down the Swamp Road before they reached you," said old MacComerou. "It's a cul-de-sac. Nobody but John Flail lives on it. But it's the only way they could have gone."

He opened the kitchen door. Inside there were those low gabbling women's voices that I had heard as I came back to the garden.

"The Swamp Road?" I said. "You mean that old wagon road about a mile or a mile and a half back, with the old ruts covered with asters and black-eyed susans, and the old sign-post beside it with the old hand-molded lead letters and the lead hands pointing, going off into deep hemlock woods? Why, that's where my car is stalled, right there at the road junction, where the road begins. And nothing turned off down it, for the last good hour."

We had entered the darkling kitchen. The murmuring women's voices which I had been hearing came from the wall beside the stove, I saw, from the receiver of the old golden-oak wall telephone, which had been left hanging. A country party line.

". . . Bobbie! He killed Bobbie! . . ."

"Oh, my poor Mrs. Wiggins! . . ."

Old Adam had paused in front of me. He caught the receiver and put it on its hook, somewhat impatiently, cutting off the gabbling, weeping voices. In the silence he turned toward me.

"You have been right at the Swamp Road junction?" he said with toothless jaws.

"I have been right at it."

"You have been at it for an hour?"

"For a good hour."

"And nothing turned off down it, you are sure of it?"

"Nothing," I said. "No car, anyway. There was a gust of wind that turned off down it. And there was a man walking away down it when I first got there. I suppose he must have turned off down it. But he had turned down it before I got there. He vanished in the woods."

"A man?" he said. "What kind of looking man?"

"He had black hair. He was rather tall, about your own height, I'd say. He was dressed in khaki pants and a blue sweat-soaked shirt, and was carrying his coat or else a sack slung over his left shoulder. He was walking with his head bent forward, at a long flat-footed shuffling Indian stride, without lifting his feet."

"John Flail," MacComerou said. "You saw him walking down Swamp Road an hour ago?"

"Yes," I said. "He was just going into the trees when I saw him. He was about two hundred yards away from me. I didn't know his name."

"John was working around my place today," he said, with a calm effort. "I didn't notice at just what precise minute he quit. He had left when that car went by is all I know. But I would have said that John Flail left here not more than ten minutes before, not more than three quarters of an hour ago, at most. . . . Of course, it may have been John Flail you saw. I wouldn't know."

Still for the moment in the darkling he stood looking at me with a pale stare, as if he were trying to look right through me. He was completely convinced in his own mind, I could see it, that the man he called John Flail, whoever he was, had not left his place here until definitely later than the time at which I had told him I had seen that figure walking away down Swamp Road.

I don't think he thought I was lying. Not that I was consciously and deliberately lying, and for a purpose. He looked as if he were just trying to figure out whether it had been a living man or an apparition I had seen. Or maybe if I was a living man or an apparition myself.

He picked up something from a shelf beside the stove—a small nickel-plated monkey wrench that I had asked for. He handed it to me.

"Wait till I've put some clothes on. I'll go along with you and see if I can help you get straightened out," he said, almost absently.

He was still thinking over a problem that I wasn't particularly interested in as yet. But I hadn't seen St. Erme going by with his pale bloodless face. And I hadn't seen that little red-eyed corkscrewed man named Doc.

But it worried MacComerou now. It worried him already. It was then that he took down his black book from the shelf beside the phone, looking through it for Dexter's number, his garage man down in New York.

He found the number, thumbing through his book. Standing in his shorts and moccasins, still dirty and sweaty from his garden, he rang the crank with a white arm like a peeled branch, to get in touch with Dexter.

That scene keeps coming back to me. In the darkling kitchen when we had entered from the garden. There had been no word of murder yet. St. Erme was a name that I had only just now heard for the first time—and he was little more than a name to MacComerou, even, I had the feeling. That little corkscrewed man had been only a man passing along the road out in front at the wheel of a big gray car, to MacComerou, as yet. To me, he had not been even that. To us both, Elinor Darrie, St. Erme's young bride-to-be, was nothing, so far. She did not exist.

There was only something vaguely ominous in the air. A phantasm that I had seen. A car that I had not seen. To MacComerou, the picture wasn't right.

I'm not sure which of those items worried him the more at the moment. What I had seen, or what I had not. But he could put in an inquiry about the car, at least.

He had laid a big silver watch down on the phone ledge. There were people talking on the line when he picked the receiver up, after ringing. Three or four voices, it sounded like, all gabbling together.

"Toll operator, please," he broke into their babble. "Oh, is that you, Mr. Unistaire? This is Mrs. Hinterzee, down the road from you! I have been trying to get you——"

"This is Professor MacComerou," he said. "Ring 5-5. I'd like to put in just a brief call to New York, if you don't mind."

"Oh, Professor MacComerou! I was going to call you up, but I was afraid you might be busy writing, and would take my head off, as you always do! Did you see a gray touring car go rushing up the road, with a terrible tramp——"

"Yes, it passed my place."

"He scared Mr. Hinterzee right out of his rocking chair! He had a terrible laugh! He ran down the poor Wigginses' dog deliberately—Bobbie, their big kind St. Bernard with the brown eyes that the children love to ride on! There was some man in the car with him who looked as if he had been struck on the head! Tell Professor MacComerou how he killed Bobbie, Mrs. Wiggins!"

"Oh, Professor, Bobbie was standing there, and he came rushing in his car! He was crouched down behind the wheel like a monkey, he had a blue hat on with a scalloped brim, he looked terrible! He swung his wheel——"

"Yes," MacComerou said with mushy quietness. "Yes, I saw him myself. Fortunate it wasn't one of your children, Mrs. Wiggins. He would have done the same to a child, no doubt of it. I have an idea that I may know who the young fellow with him was. If you will just let me have the phone three minutes, perhaps I can find out. . . .

"Toll operator? This is Whippleville 5-5. I want New York, Mordaunt 2-8385. Station-to-station call. . . ."

Dexter answered the phone himself, when the call had been put through.

It had been his car, all right. St. Erme had borrowed it to go some place with his girl. The girl had been going to drive it. But that was all that Dexter knew. . . .

That was how I happened to have heard St. Erme's name, anyway, and what the red-eyed little man with him had looked like and the license number of the car, when she flagged me on the road in the darkness down near Dead Bridegroom's Pond later, saying that her fiancé had been kidnaped and their car stolen. Rosenblatt asked me how I had known, of course.

Old Adam had continued to look through his black book while he spoke to Dexter—looking for other numbers to call up, I could guess, if the car had not been Dexter's, or the man in it with that nameless little fiend not St. Erme.

But it had been. That answered something for him. He seemed satisfied about it for the moment, as he rang off, putting his black book back up on the shelf.

"It was St. Erme, the young fellow that I thought it was," he mumbled to me, a little grimly. "I usually remember faces. There seems to have been some girl who drove him from New York. I'd rather like to know where that girl is now."

It wasn't necessary for him to tell me. That phone transmitter was quite audible, and I had ears. A good deal better ears than the average, if it was important to have him know.

(That is one thing more that a man's voice does tell about him, that I didn't consider, when thinking of Corkscrew and his voice. A man who talks loudly may be a man who does not hear so well; and the reverse for a soft-voiced man. I have always had good hearing, and I'm glad I've got it. Corkscrew, it would seem likely, from the quiet voice he had, had the hearing of a mouse.)

Anyway, I had heard what Dexter had told Mac-Comerou.

All right, so it had been St. Erme. All right, so the car was Dexter's. All right, so St. Erme's girl had been driving it. But I couldn't see what old Adam was so tense about. What had leaped into his mind.

He would like to know where St. Erme's girl was now, he said. I couldn't see for what.

I just couldn't see any connection.

"A great invention, Professor," I remarked to him. "The telephone," I explained, as he stared uncomprehendingly at me—baffled by something about me still, I could feel it. "I wish you had asked that garage man of yours if he would be willing to come up here for about twenty-five dollars and expenses, in case I can't get my car started."

"Ask Dexter to come all the way up here to get your car

started for you?" he said. "A hundred miles? Whatever put such a crazy idea into your head? It's about as crazy as I ever heard of."

He had picked up a washbasin in the sink, after hanging up the phone. He seemed annoyed at my remark, which I had intended merely as a more or less jocose reminder that what I was interested in was getting my car started. I wouldn't have expected a garage man to come up from New York, just for me. But MacComerou had to take it seriously.

"Naturally not," he said. "He would have thought I was crazy myself if I had suggested it. You don't know Dexter, Doctor. He hates the country. He likes to boast that he's never been north of the Bronx. New York has a lot of men like that. You couldn't get him up here for twenty-five hundred dollars."

"I guess I'll have to do without him, then," I said. "I doubt if I've got twenty-five hundred dollars. In cash on me, anyway."

I had taken seat on a kitchen chair while he ran water into a washbasin in the sink. He started toward me. I shifted a little on the hard seat. I had my billfold in my hip pocket with maybe forty or fifty dollars in it, of course. And there was that waddy envelope that the Buchanan housekeeper had pressed on me, on my hip, that I could feel. If there were fifty bills, and they were twenties, they would be a thousand dollars. If they were fifties—— Well, that would have been a big fee, of course, in the circumstances, considering I had done nothing. . . .

MacComerou stared at me. Then he must have seen some humor in the idea of it. In my dirty sweaty shirt and slacks, with my sweaty dirty face, looking probably to him more or less like a tramp, that I might have twenty-five hundred dollars on me. His face broke into a broad compressed grin, with crinkles about his eyes.

"I should hope not, Doctor," he said. "I shouldn't suppose you had. Is that all you're thinking about—your infernal stalled car? Don't worry, you'll doubtless get it going. A Draco '34, you say? And you've figured out that the vacuum feed line is clogged up. Well, that sounds plausible to me, not knowing anything about it. You probably don't need a garage mechanic, anyway."

He washed the garden dirt from his big brown hands with a bar of kitchen soap, dumped out the water from the basin, and filled it up again. He bent his head down and sloshed water over his face with both cupped hands, and over the top of his big pale bald head and his big brown bat ears and the back of his neck, suggling and swushing in it with his mushy toothless jaws.

If I have ever seen a picture of a six-foot hundred-and-eighty-pound bald-headed old man immersing himself in a washbasin and splashing around in it, he was it. It would have been good enough for a cartoon by Partch. He emerged, hauling a hand towel from the rack by the sink, wiping his face and hands and rubbing the rim of close-clipped white hair about his bald head, and using the damp towel then to wipe off his bony ribs and his pale gray-rurzed chest.

It seemed to make him feel a lot better.

I went to the sink and got myself a drink of water while he slipped some clothes on in the adjacent bedroom. He wasn't much of a housekeeper, old Adam, as one wouldn't expect, an old bachelor or widower, living alone this way out in the country with his garden and his thoughts.

Bachelor—I remembered that *Hom. Psych.* was dedicated to "My Sister Eva, from Whom I have Learned All that I Know about Women, or Should Care To." Having his dry little joke. But a man who would write that about his sister, even in fun, isn't the kind who ever marries. He's been born a bachelor, and will die one.

The sink looked like it, I mean. It was piled with rusty silverware and stacks of dirty cups and dishes, the remains of as many different meals, probably all of them sprouting all kinds of green and black molds. Beneath a microscope there would probably have been more different species of beautiful flowers—not to speak of bushes, shrubs, palms, and euca- lyptus trees—growing on those plates than he could grow out in his garden in a hundred years, working from dawn till dark. And all of them growing by themselves, without all that cultivation. I'll take a microscope for mine. As I had told him, I'm not a gardener.

There were some dried or rotted vegetables on the back

of the drainboard, too—a handful of withered carrots, a few potatoes that were full of sprouts, an old quarter of a cabbagehead that had half turned to slime, and a strawberry box that didn't have anything in it except stems and a mess of black mush that had once been good red berries, which nobody would eat now.

Since the therapeutic values of *Penicillium notum* have been discovered, all medical men have a profound respect for molds, even an affection. Still, that sort of slovenliness gave me not such a good opinion of old MacComerou as a person, apart from his brain. I'm not a particularly neat and fussy man, myself; and the way I leave my clothes thrown around on the floor is the bane of Mrs. Millens' existence. But I'm a surgeon, and I stick for cleanliness in things about me.

For the moment, I wondered if old Adam mightn't be a sporadic dipsomaniac—one of those men who go off on periodic sprees, letting everything go to pot around them— and mightn't be just recovering from a jag now. There are some brilliant men who do it; and not always with such destructive consequences as might be imagined, either. One of the best instructors I ever had in college had used to go off on a drunk four times a year as regularly as the seasons— would shut himself up in his room, not seeing anybody, not answering the phone except to yell into it, not eating a bite of food, not shaving or even washing his face, not even bothering to undress and go to bed, just lying sprawled in a big armchair and living whatever glorious dreams he had, all filthy and ragged and red-eyed and singing to himself, for a week or ten days at a time. And we freshmen all felt sorry for him when it was over and he had got cleaned up, because he was really a nice fellow. Maybe he was all the better for doing it, for all I know. He died young. But he might have been a murderer without it.

The water was good and cold, anyway. It was spring water piped from the water tank behind the barn, I guessed.

MacComerou came back then out of his bedroom, and he had put on a clean blue shirt, a pair of old gray flannel pants and a pair of tennis shoes. He must have guessed what I had been thinking.

"I should have apologized for the appearance of things, Doctor," he said, with a wrinkled grin. "John Flail is supposed to clean up, but if I don't keep after him he tends to let things slide. I've been working, and hadn't noticed. You found yourself a clean glass to drink out of, anyway, I hope."

"I rinsed one out," I said. "It's good cold water."

"Yes," he said. "The well's two hundred feet deep. It goes down to a rock ledge that runs under the woods in back. It's all good cold water. Perhaps," he added, with a thought, looking at me inquiringly, "you'd like something stronger, Doctor? I don't drink myself, so it didn't occur to me. But there's a small amount of medicinal rye in the cabinet, I think, which might be enough for a potion."

I told him no, thanks; that I didn't take it either—that it

might be all right in moderation for the average man, and even perhaps be a necessary release for him occasionally, but that a surgeon just couldn't touch it.

And I knew that it was true, too, what he had said about himself, that he didn't drink at all. My flitting idea that he might be a secret dipsomaniac had been senseless, when I thought it over. Even an occasional jag leaves some physical marks on a man. At the least, it speeds up the general aging process, making him look older than his years. And old MacComerou's flesh was firm and his muscles were in good tone, I would judge; and he moved limberly and strongly, like a man still in his prime. Except for his teeth, or rather his lack of them, he might have passed for no more than forty-five in the crepuscular light, and might look not so much older than that even in broad day. Though he must have been at least sixty-five, when one considered that his book had been a classic for thirty years.

There was some kind of dictating machine on a wheeled stand beside the stove, with some batteries and wires. He was dictating a sequel to *Hom. Psych.*, he told me when I asked him, and having a stenographer down in New York do it for him. He wheeled the machine out into the woodshed back of the kitchen before we started.

We went out through the kitchen door. His station wagon had a flat tire, he said, and the spare was worn out. John Flail had been supposed to patch the tube today, and had left the car standing out in front of the barn for that purpose, but apparently he hadn't got around to it. But, anyway, it wasn't far to walk, he understood, to where I had left my car.

No, I told him. Right at the Swamp Road junction. I took a banana from a box of groceries on the back porch, and peeled and ate it as we set out. I hadn't eaten anything since a cup of coffee and a doughnut at the airfield this morning before taking the plane to Burlington. And being hungry, perhaps, was a part of my splitting headache.

Old Adam still couldn't quite believe that I hadn't seen anything. He didn't doubt my word, I knew that. He didn't think I was a conscious liar. Still, he just couldn't believe it. Maybe I had seen something that I had forgotten, and would remember later. But I must have seen something, he was sure of it, whether or not I knew it.

He had brought a flashlight along, and as we went along the road he kept playing it down on the stony surface.

"What's the name of that tire with a series of S's forming the tread, do you remember?" he mumbled mushily. "Sigourney, isn't it? Sigourney Special Service Silent Silver tires, or something like that."

"That's the name, I think," I said. "Something like that. They used to advertise them a lot, all over, with a picture of a pretty girl at the wheel of a big gray sport phaeton with red cushions. But you can't get them any more."

"There are cars that are still equipped with them, nevertheless," he said, a little impatiently. "Dexter's car must have them. You can see the tracks along the road here. Still recent. Within the last hour, I would say." We stopped and squatted, and I looked.

"Where?" I said.

He pointed, touching the road with a blunt brown finger.

"The characteristic S," he said a little impatiently. "Here, and here. The car went along here. Can't you see it, Doctor? What's the matter with your eyes?"

"I've got ten-D accommodation," I said. "Emmetropic vision."

"That probably explains it," he said, getting up. "You'd see them without much trouble if you wore glasses. Never mind."

We went on, while he still played the flashlight down. Maybe he didn't believe me, and thought that I really did need glasses—that I was just being vain about my eyes, with one of those small vanities some men have. He must have known what 10-D accommodation meant, and emmetropic vision. He knew more ophthalmology than an oculist. More anatomy than an anatomist, even though he wasn't a medical doctor. I really have the eyes of a fly. Scheduled for flight surgeon in the Navy air arm, two stripes and a half, next month, after battling for three years to get my release from St. John's and S. and P.—they need surgeons, too—if he wanted to know it. I've got eyes.

I figured that he must have hypnotized himself into seeing those tracks. He knew the car had gone by, and so there must be tracks, and so he saw them. But I just couldn't see them. The road was so hard and dry. No dust to take an imprint. Brown hard clay earth, and flint, and granite. Dry.

But the gray murder car had gone along here all right, tracks or not. He was right about that. We came to the eyeless house with the fallen roof that stood off in the weeds, or to just this side of it, where I had heard the croaking in the ditch, after I had picked up that damned hat and thrown it away and had started to walk on.

There was no croaking in the ditch now, but there was blood upon the road beside it. Drops and little pools. It glistened in the moving of MacComerou's flashlight, as he stopped beside me, with his bald head bent, his shoulders bent over, staring at it. It was there, all right, and I must have walked right through it without noticing it, as I came past, for there was the circular print of a crepe-soled shoe in the blood, and it was mine.

We went down off the road into the high weeds of the ditch, where the trail of blood led, and found Flail. He was lying there, supine among the roots of the weeds on the damp earth at the bottom of the ditch, with his black Indian eyes in his dark Indian face staring up at us, and his lank black Indian hair forming a kind of pillow beneath his head. He was still wearing his sweat-stained blue workshirt and khaki pants, and his soft-soled mocpacs in which he had been walking along at his shuffling shambling flat-footed stride, as I had seen him in my vision at sunset down the Swamp Road, with his coat that he had been carrying over his shoulder clutched in his right hand now, and twisted around it and his arm.

"Don't touch him, Doctor!" MacComerou cautioned me, with his jaw working.

I hadn't any mind to. I wasn't the official medical examiner. Or coroner, as it is in Connecticut. Only to lay a hand on his heart, to make sure that he was dead.

"Who is he? Flail?" I said.

MacComerou nodded inarticulately. "You didn't know him, did you? No, of course not. You heard me speak of him. Yes, John Flail. He left my place only about ten minutes before that car went by. That devil must have struck him deliberately."

That was what it looked like. He had been hit and smashed, as hard as a heavy car can smash a man. Half the bones in his body must have been broken at the impact. I could see tire marks on his shirt, those "SSSS" mark of Sigourney Silent Specials, which I had been unable to see on the road.

It had been a wonder he had lived for thirty seconds, crushed like that. But he had lived, to drag himself down into the weeds of the ditch, with his coat still clutched in his hand. He had probably died about half an hour ago, about the time I had passed this way. It had been, more than likely, his last groan or death rattle that I had heard—that inhuman croaking in the ditch. A sound that I had thought of as definitely not human. Because it had been human only in part.

A hit-and-run. It looked bad, the way those tires had gone over him. Still, it was manslaughter, and not murder, without proof of premeditation, without knowing just how it had been done. And that was proof and knowledge, I thought, which it would be hard to get, since Flail had apparently been walking here alone. Whether he had known who had killed him or not, there was no way to say.

It wasn't definitely murder, anyway. It wasn't murder yet. It wasn't murder stalking in the night, black, bloody, with a knife. It wasn't the damp sawdust heaps. It wasn't terror.

Not then. Not yet. It was a hit-and-run, and nasty, but that was all, as I could see it. Death had just gone by.

"The police will have to be notified," said MacComerou, with compressed lips. "They'll have to have a complete description of Dexter's car, too, and of that red-eyed man who was driving it with St. Erme. They will want a statement from you as to how we found him here, Doctor. You can tell them that you never saw him before, of course."

"I thought that I saw him walking away down the Swamp Road at sunset," I pointed out. "I should mention that."

MacComerou, squatting on the other side of the body of John Flail, looked at me for a moment.

"If I were you," he said, "I think I would not mention having seen any phantasms, Doctor."

He arose, stepping back, and began to play his flashlight up and down the ditch.

"After all, it isn't pertinent," he commented, with a calm effort. "Phantasms and mental illusions aren't of any benefit to the police, I don't think. Even our own personal deductions or assumptions aren't particularly wanted by them, since those are liable to be colored by our own mental slants. You found John Flail's body here with me. Neither of us touched it. That's what they want to know. We can assume for ourselves that he was struck by a car coming up behind him, while he was shambling along with his coat over his shoulder, as in your vision of him prior to his death. We can assume that, after being struck, he crawled down from the road into the ditch where we found him. But the police can make their own examinations and deductions. They are trained for it.

"Of course," he added, "if we should happen to discover any positive piece of additional information, it is proper and even necessary to bring it to their attention."

In the weeds then, a dozen steps farther, as he went down it with his flash, he found the blue mutilated hat.

I went down to join him where he was crouching, looking at it. He hadn't touched it. He was just squatting, working his toothless gums together, staring down at it in the flashlight's beam where it lay in the damp soil, among the weeds at the bottom of the ditch.

It had startled and even terrified him. It was such a damned-looking thing, little wonder. He lifted his eyes, fixed and pale among their wrinkles, staring at me all over again. I could almost feel him putting a tape measure around my head.

"I'd like to know how it got there," he said, as I squatted down beside him. "I'd like damned well to know."

"I threw it here," I said.

"You threw it here?" he said.

"I found it on the road," I said.

"Oh," he said. "You found it on the road?"

"Yes," I said. "I noticed it and picked it up. It used to be a hat of mine."

His lips worked together without opening, without a sound. But I knew what he was saying, anyway. He was saying, "Oh, it used to be a hat of yours?"

"Yes," I said, picking it up and opening it to the sweatband. "Haxler's on Fifth Avenue. It used to have my initials on it, too, you can see. It's my own old hat, no question of it. My maid must have given it to the Salvation Army, or maybe put it out with the trash. I suppose it's going to be pretty hard to trace."

The flashlight lay upon his knees. If I had shrunk in that moment to five feet three, and had grown a beard and long matted auburn hair, small red eyes and pointed teeth, I don't think it would have surprised him.

He got up with his knees a little wobbly under him.

"Let's go," he said. "We might as well see about that car of yours, before I call the police."

Four or five hundred yards farther on—along that narrow high-crowned ditch-bordered road, with the old unbroken stone fences on either side that were overgrown with

their great vine ropes and warty leaves, and woods beyond—
we came to the bend. And around it, a hundred feet ahead,
there was the old Draco coupe standing where I had left it,
at the road fork.

We walked toward it. MacComerou had still been flashing his light in circles on the road for those Sigourney tread
tracks that I hadn't seen. But when he saw the car standing
there, he lost interest in trying to pick them up again. Perhaps he hadn't seen them any more now, either.

The battered old coupe was there. It was just there. In
the middle of the narrow road, and right across the entrance
to the Swamp Road, beside that three-armed sign. No car
could have gone by. It just could not have gone by, without
going down into the ditch and leaving a swath through the
weeds, and maybe knocking down a section of stone wall,
and a lot of other things. It couldn't have gone on past me
toward Stony Falls, and it couldn't have turned off down the
Swamp Road. MacComerou could see that.

He didn't say anything for a good minute, trying to think
it out. I didn't say anything, either. I didn't want to rub it in.
I opened the coupe door, turned on the headlights, and got
out my flashlight. I lifted up the hood.

"Perhaps you were mistaken about the time you were
here, Doctor?" he said.

But he didn't say it with any great conviction. He knew
that I had been here, as I had said.

"From sunset," I told him, "till I came and spoke to you
in your garden. You remember?"

"Yes," he said. "I remember."

I loosened the feed-line nut with the little monkey wrench he had lent me, and unscrewed it the rest of the way with my fingers. It had just needed a start. I bent up the end of the copper tube, put my mouth to it, and sucked on it. Some dirt or lint came out, and then a mouthful of raw gasoline. That was all there was to it. I spat the gasoline out, with the taste still in my teeth. I took out the little filter screen and blew through it, put it back in, and connected the line again, tightening the nut with my fingers and the wrench. I closed down the hood again, while insects sang, and MacComerou stood watching me.

"You aren't a very imaginative man, are you, Dr. Riddle?" he said.

"What is there to imagine?"

"Most men have some imagination," he said. "A little, anyway."

"Maybe it's my hard luck," I told him. "A screw missing. But maybe there's enough imagination in the world already without what I might contribute. That ought to have done the trick, Professor. Here's your wrench, before I forget it. And thanks."

"Maybe I had better give it to you," he said.

He stood looking at me, holding it.

"No, thanks," I said. "I wouldn't want to take it. I don't expect to run into any more trouble."

Insects hummed in the darkness, and there was an owl howling in the woods down there on Swamp Road. I stepped down along the road with my flash to find the crank that I had heaved at that yellow rattler. It was lying across the ruts where it had bounced. I picked it up. In one of the ruts my flashlight showed the snake, lying straight as a ribbon, with its head smashed down on a stone, with its long hooked fangs extruding from its pulped jaws, and its hard eyes cold.

My quick, hard throw had nailed it, though I hadn't realized it. It hadn't slipped away, too quick to see. That is a hard thing to do, even for a snake. It had slid down beneath grass, trying to cover up, but that was all it could do. The mortal blow had hit it, and it was finished. And so it had lain there, hard-eyed and dying, with what thoughts in its reptile brain, hell knew. It would certainly have liked to bite me, but it hadn't had the chance.

I turned, with the crank in my hand. MacComerou was standing there behind me. He had a twelve-pound rock in his hand, which he had picked up.

"That's all right," I said. "It's dead."

His toothless gums were working a little. His bat ears seemed to quiver. He tossed the rock off into the weeds, and took a breath.

In the woods the owl howled again.

I got in behind the wheel and snapped on the switch. I had worked up a little battery juice with all the cranking I had done before; and when I stepped on the starter now the engine turned over, caught, and held its tone.

I laid the crank across my knees so that MacComerou

could sit beside me. But it was only a short distance back, and he didn't bother to get in. He stood on the running board, holding to the windshield post and breathing in the refreshing night air, while we rode back, past the eyeless house and the place where John Flail's body lay in the weeds, and on down to where the stone fences ended in the privet of his place, to his drive.

He would have to notify the state police at their nearest barracks, at Readsfield twenty miles over beyond Stony Falls, in regard to having found John Flail killed by that hit-and-run, and have them send out an alarm for Dexter's car and the driver. But it might be a couple of hours before they got down themselves. In the meantime there was no particular use of my waiting, if I wanted to get back to New York tonight, he thought. I could give him my address, in case they wanted a deposition from me. But they might not need any statement from me at all, since it would be merely corroborative of his that we had found Flail there.

I agreed with him. I'm not a man to dodge issues. But I hadn't been a witness to the event itself, any more than he had, and I had not even seen the car go by, nor seen that red-eyed man. It would be just a waste of time for me to wait around.

I gave him my address at St. John's, where I should more likely to be found than at 511 West, when I had dropped him at the mailbox beside his drive. The phoebes which were nesting in the paper box stirred, I thought, but they did not come fluttering out against my face this time as when I had first appeared. Perhaps they can't see at night.

For a moment old Adam stood watching me as I started on, not quite believing yet that I was real, somehow, I think. Then he turned and went striding up the driveway along which that gaunt hoarse twanging cat had fled from me in the twilight, as if he wanted to dismiss me from his mind.

Three or four miles down the road there was a low flat-roofed California-style bungalow standing in among fields at my left. It had wide plate glass windows that were all lit up inside, with red shades half pulled down; and I could hear a jukebox or a loud victrola playing some crazy tune inside.

There was a wide circular driveway that went in, around in front of it. It looked as if it might be a teahouse or something. I swung in, with a squeal of tires, between two low cobblestone gateposts that were placed wide apart, to see if I could get a cup of coffee and a sandwich, for my head was still splitting.

There was some splintered kindling under wheel as I came around the circle. The figure of something—animal or human—swung into my headlights on the driveway in front of the porch steps, crouching on all fours among the debris. It wore a leopard skin and a pale purple gown, and had a feather duster fastened to its stern like a rooster's tail. It leaped up with a rabbit scream and away from in front of my lights as I came around at it, and went rushing up the steps like something in a surrealist's dream, and in through the front door, leaving the door open behind it.

I went on around the drive, and out again. Fast. It was still a damned nightmare road. I was out through the cobbled gateposts and on it again when that incredible figure appeared in the lighted doorway of the bungalow, with something in its hands that looked like a shotgun. It was, for I saw a flash and heard a roar, and saw another flash and heard a roar, as I went on down the road, away.

A mile and a half or two farther, I saw four or five small gnomelike figures looming in the road in front of me. They rushed, fleeing to the roadside, before my headlights, and from the roadside I heard a man shout.

I slowed as I came abreast. There was a shingled old house in at my right, with a small light in it, beyond a hedge, standing among low broad trees that had the shape of apple trees. The figure of a man stood pressed back against the hedge beside the road, with four or five children clustered about him, those figures that I had seen. He seemed to be trying to embrace the shoulders of all of them, drawing them in to him, with his staring face upon me.

Just the picture of a poor father, frightened, trying to protect his children from something intangible in the night. Fathers have been doing it since the days of the saber-tooth tiger, or the race would not be here.

"Route 7?" I called to him.

"Keep on, mister!" he cried quaveringly.

But it wasn't so much a direction, it seemed like, as an

adjuration and supplication to me to go on. To remove my image out of his life and his quiet orchard peace.

Two miles farther on, down that dark winding nightmare way, a lamp shone from the curtainless windows of a rickety shack house at my left, close beside the road. The front door opened as my car approached, throwing light out onto the tumbledown porch. A thick-set bowlegged man in an undershirt and a pair of overalls, with a broken nose and a shock of hair, stood behind the screen door in the rectangle of light, holding a big yellowish airedale-collie mongrel by the collar. He pushed the screen door open and loosed the dog with a gruff laconic grunt as I came by, and the beast shot out with a deep-throated growl, in a slavering rush at my wheels.

For a quarter mile or more it kept beside me down the stony winding road, snarling and foaming and snapping at my tires, savage and murderous, hating me with its life. It's often said that dogs, children, and lunatics have an infallible instinct for character. If that big, savage brute had anything to say about it, I was Jack the Ripper.

Yet I had been through blood, and perhaps that was what kept him at it. There had been Flail's blood on the road, and the blood of Wiggins' St. Bernard in front of his place that I had passed. And perhaps there had been St. Erme's blood all along the road, though I didn't know about that yet. But that dog knew, or else he just hated me.

A nightmare road. I might have dreamed it, from the time that I had turned off onto it at sunset, with a splitting head. Phantasms and eyeless houses and a red-eyed rattle-snake and a crazy hat of mine; and old Adam MacComerou staring at me through the garden dusk as I appeared, as if he couldn't believe that I was real; and then a dead man in the ditch whose last breath I had heard. And skittering surrealistic lunatics and a terrified father clutching his children as if I might eat them, and now this damned slavering dog that would tear my throat out if he could.

All down the nightmare road. But the road was real. I didn't dream it. And I knew that I was real. I'll stick to that . . .

The big snarling rushing mongrel left off finally. The road was empty again. I only wanted to come to the end of it. I wanted to meet nothing more till I got out onto the wide smooth concrete of Route 7, and was headed down fast for home.

Yet it had been all merely something amorphous and intangible—to me, and to everyone else—so far. There had been only a weird horn, and a gray car, and an ugly little demon at the wheel driving it and laughing, and a stricken man beside him who had looked like death. A big tail-wagging dog that had been run down, and some splintered easel frames on a surrealist's drive. Just the body of John Flail, smashed on the road, which old MacComerou and I had found. MacComerou hadn't even been sure that St. Erme had been hurt, when that car had gone by—it had been the sight, more, of that horrible little man with him which had worried him. He hadn't even been sure that it had been St. Erme, until he had called up Dexter, after I got there.

All ugly, and a little frightening. Sinister was the word for it. The women in their kitchens were discussing it over their phones. The party wire that ran along the road above me had been humming all the way as I drove down. They had all heard MacComerou phoning the state police by this time, telling about the finding of John Flail's body, and giving the number of the car which he had learned.

All a little frightening. But not yet deliberate murder. Not the terror yet. The first man killed with the sawtooth knife had not yet been found.

He had to be found to make it real. They didn't know, in those houses I had passed, that before they had put out their lights, if they were late stayers-up, or before they had been asleep very long, even if they got to bed early, all of them—all the men of them, and all the whole countryside for ten miles around—would be aroused and getting out their lanterns and flashlights, their cars and guns, and going down to the Swamp Road to hunt along it, and through the woods on either side, and around the old sawmill where the road petered out to corduroy and muck-land, looking for red-eyed little Corkscrew, the man with the matted auburn hair, the man with the dog teeth and the pointed ear, who had killed Inis St. Erme and used surgical instruments on his body, and killed old Professor

MacComerou and hidden him away in the tons of damp rotted sawdust down below the sawmill. The man who has struck down Unistaire and perhaps Trooper Stone and Quelch and Rosenblatt himself by now. And how many others out in the darkness where they are hunting him there is no saying yet.

He needed to be found, that first one of them, to make it real. St. Erme needed to be found . . .

A quarter mile down the road from where that slavering dog had left off, I saw the white-coated form of the girl, pressed back against the roadside rock wall, in my headlights, scratched and burr-covered from her hiding and her running, white-faced and panicky, with her great dark eyes, signaling to me imploringly to stop. Her car had been stolen and her fiancé kidnaped.

She turned and fled from me when I told her to get in. But I jumped out and caught her, and got her into the car. And when she had quieted down a little, she told it. She and Inis St. Erme had been on their way to be married. They had picked up a tramp on the road. The tramp had attacked St. Erme, and had stalked her through the woods while she hid, and had then gone on up the road that I had come down. Had I seen him?

No, I hadn't seen him. But I would get her to the police.

I drove on down the road with her to the parking place overlooking Dead Bridegroom's Pond, and got out and felt the grass and weeds there. And it was murder I had put my hand in.

I brought her back here to MacComerou's.

There was a police car on the road in front already when I arrived with her. I drove halfway up the graveled drive to the kitchen door, and pocketed my keys this time when I got out. MacComerou's station wagon, out in front of the big white barn at the end of the drive, was out of commission with its flat tire; so I wasn't blocking it for him. I don't like to block people.

A kerosene lamp had been lit in the kitchen and there was a whiter light in the living room beyond. A state trooper was inside, a sandy-haired man with a broad, smiling face. He was just finishing a phone call in the kitchen when we entered, and he nodded to us as he put up the receiver, with his meaningless professional smile.

"Trooper Stone," he introduced himself. "What can I do for you people?"

He led us into the living room, old-fashioned and a little dusty, but where the green-shaded gasoline lamp on the table gave a better light, and there were places to sit down. Sitting straight-backed on the horsehair sofa, gazing at him with anxious intentness, she told him her story, as if she were reciting her Latin lesson again in a high-school class.

Adding a few details, which she had forgotten, to what she had already told me. But I have included them. Trooper Stone's smile did not change.

"Your car's been found," he said. "Mr. St. Erme wasn't in it. That's really a good indication. If he had been badly hurt or—well, dead—this man Doc would have just left him. It looks more as if he had forced Mr. St. Erme to go along with him at the point of a knife, in a crazy kidnaping attempt. But he can't have gone far with him, and when he realizes he is cornered he will probably give up. Lieutenant Rosenblatt and Professor MacComerou are down there now, with Mr. Unistaire from the next house below. The lieutenant sent me back to phone for more troopers. It won't be long."

"Where was the car found?" I said.

"Down at the end of the Swamp Road," he told me.

"The Swamp Road?"

"Yes," he said. "Down past John Flail's. You know, the old wagon road about a mile and a quarter up from here. It's the only side road off there is all the way along from Whippleville to Stony Falls."

"Yes, I know the road you mean," I said.

"There's nothing to do but wait and not be too worried, Miss Darrie," he said. "The radio doesn't seem to have any batteries, but there are a couple of magazines to read. Or some books, or there's a copy of the Danbury paper on the desk, it looks like. I'll make some coffee."

But she had left her glasses in the car when they had got out down at Dead Bridegroom's Pond, and she couldn't read very well without them. At Stone's urging, she picked up an old copy of a picture magazine from the table, and began looking through it, to pass the moments of suspenseful waiting.

I followed Stone out into the kitchen after we had got her settled.

"You live around here, Dr. Ridder?" he asked me, making coffee.

"Riddle," I said. "No, I live in New York. I'm on my way down from Vermont. I wonder when that car passed me."

"You saw it passing you?"

"No," I said. "I didn't see it."

"I thought you meant it passed you," he said. "We're interested in people who saw it and the man who was driving it."

"I can't give you any help there," I told him.

Stone and his commanding officer, Lieutenant Rosenblatt, had already been on their way down from Readsfield, it seemed, when Professor MacComerou had called up the barracks there, reporting the hit-and-run and giving the number of Dexter's car and describing the man with the torn ear who had been driving it. They had arrived half an hour, or not much more, after I had left.

They had come down, as part of a routine patrol, to question John Flail about his brother Pete, who had been released two weeks ago from the Wethersfield pen after serving three years of his term for manslaughter for killing a man in a drunken brawl in Bridgeport, and who hadn't reported on probation. The Bridgeport police had asked them to inquire, having had a rumor that Pete had left the state for the West Coast. The radio in their car had been out of commission, and so they hadn't learned the information which Professor MacComerou had phoned in, on their way down. Not finding John Flail at his little tar-paper shack down on the Swamp Road when they got there, they had come on out again and down to Professor MacComerou's here, to see if he knew anything about Pete.

Professor MacComerou hadn't known anything about Pete Flail. He hadn't heard John mention him and was sure that Pete hadn't returned home, anyway, or he would have seen him. He told them about John Flail.

MacComerou had learned when he phoned Readsfield that they were on their way, and would probably stop in at his place to phone when they didn't find John Flail. He had coffee ready for them. They had had a cup, and then had gone on down with him to where Flail had been struck. In their police spotlight they had picked up a rock on the road about the size to fit a man's fist—a thing that MacComerou and I had missed—that had blood and black hairs on it.

Examining Flail's body in the ditch, they had found that he hadn't been killed just by a hit-and-run driver. The back of his head had been smashed in, in a way that nothing on a car could have done, and the mark of the blow had fitted the stone they had found on the road. It looked as if he had been killed by someone who had come up softly behind him as he was shambling on the road, before he had been run over and his chest crushed and the bones of his body broken.

After examing the terrain, and finding the circular track of a crepe-soled shoe in the blood and an old cut-up hat, they had taken Flail's body on down the Swamp Road to his shack.

Just a little beyond, the road was mucky. There were Sigourney Silent Special tire tracks in the mire. Rosenblatt and he had noticed them before in their headlights, Stone told me, when they had been to Flail's to inquire about his brother, but there having been nothing to connect them with the minor mission they had been on, they had not investigated them at that time. Now they went on down the road, and a little farther on, where the road petered out beyond the old sawmill, they had found the gray Cadillac phaeton with its red cushions.

With blood on its right-hand door and the cushions, and a fine-woven Panama trampled in the mire beside it. With big shapeless tracks, as though the little killer had wrapped his feet in strips of cloth or bags, around the car, going back up toward John Flail's shack and going back again. And going nowhere.

"The girl's lucky to be alive," Stone told me privately, from the corner of his changeless smile. "I wouldn't give anything for St. Erme. This guy is just a crazy killer. He probably intended to pitch St. Erme's body down into some deep ravine along the road, when he came to it, and keep on going. Only he turned off down this side road by mistake, probably thinking it would get him out somewhere by a short cut. He's either a stranger to the country or some guy who hasn't lived around here in a long time and has kind of forgotten it. If he'd kept on, he'd have got out onto 49A at Stony Falls and maybe fifty miles away before we got the alarm. Of course the car would have been found eventually, in any case. You couldn't miss it. But if he had abandoned it beforehand, on the edges of some town, it might have been a lot harder to have found *him*. He's hid St. Erme's body, of course, so we can't prove murder on him when we catch him. But it's murder, anyway, with John Flail."

I knew already that it was murder. I had put my hand in it nine miles down beside the road. If I had examined John Flail's body at all when MacComerou and I found him, I suppose I should have known it then.

"Funny that I thought your name was Ridder," Stone said, as he took the coffee off the stove and got cups—of which there was now a clean supply, I was glad to see, the dirty dishes in the sink having been washed, and the sink cleaned up. "I thought maybe you were a member of the old Ridder family who used to live around here. This place used to belong to old Henry Ridder, the father of young Harry Ridder that killed all his family with an ax seven years ago, and then disappeared. People always thought down in the swamp. You may have read about it in the papers.

"No one's lived here ever since. You couldn't get them to. When I heard last March that Professor Adam MacComerou, the famous murder psychologist, was buying the place, I almost split a gut. I've got a cousin who is the Fryatt Farm Agency representative in Readsfield. The old man bought it sight unseen, George told me, just from pictures in the New York offices, like half of them do, though George got his commission, anyway. Professor MacComerou probably thought he was getting a bargain at the price. Of course he's fixed it up on the outside, new paint and new roofs and all, and clearing out the weeds. But I wouldn't live here for a farm myself. There's always just the chance that young Harry might come back. Funny my thinking that your name was Ridder, Doc."

"No," I said. "My name is Riddle. Dr. Henry N. Riddle, Jr., of New York. I don't like to be called Doc."

There was a car that came in the drive outside behind mine, and a man came into the kitchen. He was a tall thin man with three hairs plastered over the top of his head, wearing a high starched collar and a black bow tie.

He was Mr. Quelch, he said, the postmaster at Whippleville, down on Route 7. He had heard over the phone about that gray car. It had stopped at the post office about 7:36, with a dark-complected fellow in a Panama hat and a girl in blue-rimmed glasses, looking for a picnic spot, and that hairy fellow in the back seat. The dark-complected fellow had reminded him a good deal of Two-finger Pete Flail, only a lot better dressed, and looking more intelligent and high class.

Well, he hadn't been Pete, Stone told him. He had been a man named St. Erme from New York.

No, he knew he wasn't Pete, said Mr. Quelch. He was a

lot older fellow. But he sure knew how to pick the girls, or maybe let them pick him. The girl who had been driving that big gray car had sure been a knockout, a lalapalooza, she had been pretty enough to eat—

She was in the living room now, Stone told him, which cut his garrulity short. Straightening his bow tie with both hands, Mr. Quelch cut a brief caper. He proceeded on into the living room, smoothing down the three hairs on his head . . .

Quelch reported the conversation he had had at the post office with St. Erme, in great detail, to Lieutenant Rosenblatt later, when Rosenblatt was interviewing everybody; and it's all down in the book. If it could have been called a conversation, and not a monologue. The only value to it, perhaps, is that Quelch was the last man to talk to St. Erme, and perhaps to see him alive. Except for Corkscrew, of course, who saw him to the death, and may have exchanged a few quick fierce words with him beside the car, before his dying scream.

Quelch saw Corkscrew, too, with a great deal of detail, while they were parked there in front of the post office. Everything except Corkscrew's torn ear, since it was on the other side from him, and Corkscrew's height, since Corkscrew was seated, and was a man of normal height from the waist, with arms even a little long A rather observant man— Quelch. He saw about as much as I might have seen myself, perhaps.

However, I have never seen him.

Stone was going back down on the Swamp Road to rejoin Rosenblatt, Professor MacComerou, and Unistaire, after we had finished our coffee, and I asked permission to accompany him. Quelch was a good man to leave St. Erme's young bride with—a comical fellow, a 1910-style lady-killer, with a flood of conversation and moldy jokes to keep her mind off the dark matters down there by the old sawmill. I head her laughing spontaneously at something he had said as we got in Stone's police car out in front and started off. She didn't know how black it was then, of course.

She doesn't know now. And won't know till she wakes.

Or ever, if I can keep her from it.

He crept up behind John Flail and killed him with a stone blow on the back of the head, and then ran over his body.

He killed or mortally wounded St. Erme with a knife down there beside Dead Bridegroom's Pond, then raced up the road past here with St. Erme's body in the seat beside him, turned off down the Swamp Road, clubbed and bludgeoned him before he was quite dead—then or earlier—and cut off his right hand, then heaved him into the swamp.

He killed MacComerou, who had got too close to him in some way, it seems, and then killed Unistaire when Unistaire ran screaming to report it.

He may have killed Quelch—there was that scream from Quelch an hour ago, sounding through the woods back of the house here, somewhere down toward John Flail's. He may have killed Rosenblatt as well, though Rosenblatt was armed with a police gun, when Rosenblatt went rushing out to see.

And how many others, I don't know. They have brought in the dogs from somewhere now. But they will do no good.

Unistaire, the refugee Basque artist who lived down the road—a dapper, bright-eyed little man, with black hair wetted and neatly combed, and perfectly normal in a bright Hawaiian sport shirt and orange slacks and rope-soled espadrilles when I met him down on the road beyond John Flail's with MacComerou and Rosenblatt—said, as we stood talking, after Stone and I had arrived down there:

"This is definitely a surrealistic murder. It is the murder of a genius. It has symbolism. You, Lieutenant Rosenblatt and Trooper Stone, are too much the routine policemen, thinking only in terms of moronic killers for gain, to understand it. What you both need is to wear a leopard skin, a chiffon nightgown, and a feather duster on your tail, and dance the beautiful dance of the corkscrew and the bottle. You, Dr. Riddle, are too pragmatic and unimaginative to understand it. What you need is to believe with all your soul in phantasms which cannot possibly exist. Even you, Professor MacComerou, have discontinued sending John Flail daily for a quart of warm rich creamy yellow milk from my beautiful Jersey cow with the great liquid eyes, and it is milk alone which nourishes the psychological brain."

And he laughed mockingly at all of us.

"A surrealistic murder!" he said with delight. "And it takes a surrealist to interpret and explain it. I have the key.

I understand the symbolism. I will interpret and explain it. Give me a quarter head of moldy cabbage, a wig, a pair of glass eyeballs, an old umbrella, a dressmaker's form, a cube of ice, and a copy of *Mein Kampf* with the title printed in red letters, and I will put the picture together and explain it."

Unistaire had nothing on his mind. Nothing whatever.

I know that, and I will always know it. He was only mildly cracked. There are always men who gather, like flies to carrion, around a murder that way, drinking in the excitement, posing and posturing in their little vanity, trying to declaim how they would solve it, strutting and preening themselves on how much more brilliant they are than the police, as well as the dead flesh which has been murdered. Or perhaps Unistaire really was badly cracked, and really believed that a surrealist picture would explain it.

Corkscrew may have been listening and may have believed him, anyway. We found Unistaire, soon after he had found MacComerou, with his throat cut, in the deep damp sawdust pits that had been there a hundred years.

That is, I found Unistaire.

"You were with Professor MacComerou when John Flail's body was found, too, weren't you, Doctor?" Rosenblatt said to me.

"Yes," I said. "We found it together. Blood upon the road, leading off into the ditch. I didn't know who he was, of course. I had never seen him before. I had passed by a little while before and had heard a groaning, but hadn't realized it was a man. I was thinking about that damned hat that I had picked up. And then, too, I had a headache. When MacComerou and I came back to get my car started, we saw the blood and found Flail."

"By 'that damned hat,' you mean your own hat that you had found, Doctor?" said Rosenblatt, looking at me with his wrinkled pugdog face.

"Yes," I said. "My own hat that I had found."

"I almost wish you hadn't told me it was your hat," said Rosenblatt.

I didn't doubt he did.

"Sorry," I said, "to spoil your fun."

"You seem to be pretty good at finding bodies, Doctor. You found St. Erme's, too, didn't you?"

"I didn't know that it was his. A dead body has no individuality to me. I never saw him alive."

"No," said Rosenblatt with a sigh. "I know that. I know that so damned well. If you say it again, I'll go corkscrew myself. You had never seen St. Erme, and you had never seen this red-eyed little Doc. You were at the Swamp Road all during the murder hour, during the time he drove this car down here, and you didn't see either of them, or the car."

"That's right," I said. "I'll stick to that."

"Maybe I'd just better write it off at that," said Rosenblatt. "Case closed, and forget it. Dr. Riddle never saw St. Erme or Doc. So what else is there to know?"

But that was while we were kneeling over poor Unistaire's

body, and after MacComerou. St. Erme had to be found first to make it real. St. Erme needed to be found.

I was the one who found him—St. Erme—as it happened. Or found all that has been found yet, or that perhaps ever will be found. All but his right hand.

There was that gray gabardine-clad arm in the swamp, extruding from the muck, among the tall water grasses. We were all going through the swamp in a widening circle—Rosenblatt and Stone and the other troopers who had come down, and MacComerou and Unistaire and the other men from the surrounding countryside who had come down in their cars, leaving them parked all the way along Swamp Road, and I. We had formed this line, spreading out on both sides of the road from where the big gray car had stopped on the corduroy. And in my flashlight then I found him.

"Here's something!" I raised my voice.

It wasn't very far away from the car. Only a few rods out in the swamp. He hadn't bothered or else hadn't had time to bury it. It looked as if he had hauled the body out, and then taken only a few plunging steps with it on his shoulders, and heaved it off in haste. There weren't any tracks—the soil was too watery, and the muck had closed in. The body had settled down in the muck and grasses, all except that arm.

I reached for the hand to pull it up by, as the others came gathering around. But there wasn't any hand. That was the most sickening feeling that I have ever had, as a student or in practice, or previously during tonight, or ditch. It was worse than finding John Flail's body in the ditch. It was worse than that blood on the road beside Dead Bridegroom's Pond. It was worse than Unistaire later, almost beside me, looking at me with his bright mouse eyes that tried to say something, but couldn't, as I bent over him in the avalanching sawdust which already had buried old MacComerou beneath tons.

There wasn't any hand. St. Erme's right hand was missing. That was the shock of it, because I knew from the description of him that he had one, somewhere.

Rosenblatt helped me to get hold of the body by the shoulders and pull it out. With some of the other men, we carried it to the corduroy, in front of the gray Cadillac's headlights.

He was wearing his fine silky gabardine suit and his fine white silk shirt with the gold love-knot cuff links. His purse was in his pocket, though emptied of all papers and money. There was only a bill from the President Hotel in New York, stamped paid that morning, in one of his hip pockets. He had probably paid it and stuck it there, while he was waiting for Elinor Darrie to come in Dexter's big sport phaeton and pick him up. It was the only thing with his name on it that the killer had overlooked. Every other paper and mark of identification was gone, absolutely.

And his ring hand, with the ring on it.

That wasn't quite the worst, of course. Half the bones in his body seemed smashed and broken. There weren't any tire tracks on his clothing, though; only the black swamp muck. Unless he had been stripped and run over, and then dressed again—which would seem incredible—it must have been done with repeated and furious blows with a padded crank handle or some other padded bludgeon. And—by the evidence of the contusions—done before he was quite dead.

But worst, perhaps, was the thing that had been done with his skull. The skin of his forehead had been sliced across with a surgical scalpel, or else an extraordinarily sharp knife, and peeled down over his black staring eyes. Other things had been done with that scalpel to his face, too, around his mouth and ears. And there was the circular mark of a trephine on his skull where someone had tried a crude trepanning job on him. Or had begun it, though that someone hadn't got very far along with it when something must have frightened him.

St. Erme had to be found to make the horror real. And he had been found.

I had to make the preliminary observations. I was there, and I was the only doctor at hand. The old coroner had gone into the army; and the new coroner who had been appointed to replace him was eighty years old, and hadn't yet been got out of his bed over beyond Stony Falls. Country districts never are well supplied with doctors, anyway. Not enough for the living, much less for the dead. So it was up to me to examine and say what had been done to him. I didn't like it.

Rosenblatt knew some anatomy and elementary medical science, of course, and MacComerou knew a lot. More than a lot of doctors themselves, maybe. And almost any man knows of his own experience that ordinarily a man has two hands. But St. Erme had only one. His right hand had been cut off at the wrist, which was what had got me down, even more than those other things.

"Someone started to use a surgical trepan on him," said Rosenblatt to MacComerou, ignoring me. "Some man with a certain amount of medical knowledge, wouldn't you say, Professor?"

He was already ignoring me. Maybe he had begun to almost from the first. When I had told him that I hadn't seen that car or Corkscrew. When I had identified the sawtooth blue hat as mine.

"A trephine, not a trepan, Lieutenant," I said.

"What's the difference, Professor?" said Rosenblatt, ignoring me.

MacComerou, kneeling across from me with his big brown bat ears standing out on his head, with his pale gaze on me, let me reply.

"A trepan is an old-style instrument that nobody uses any more," I said. "A trephine makes a circular incision like this. The man who did this knows less about surgery than I do about motor mechanics. It is terribly crudely done. It wasn't an operation with any sense to it, either. It looks like some crazy man trying to get an idea out of St. Erme's head with an auger after he was dead."

"I suppose you have a trephine yourself, Doctor?" Rosenblatt said.

"I'd hate to be without one."

"What about his right hand, Doctor? What happened to it?"

"I wish I knew. I don't doubt that it's around here some place, and that we had a damned sight better find it. That's what makes me sick."

"I mean, how was the hand severed?"

"It was cut off with a surgical saw," I said.

"I suppose you have a saw, too?"

"I have a full set of tools," I said. "I'm a good mechanic at my trade. Or I did have them, in the luggage compartment of my car."

"You had them while you were parked right at the entrance to the Swamp Road during the murder hour, and so on?"

"And so on," I said . . .

It's funny how a man sticks things away in his hip pocket. Some men stick a lodge card or a driver's license, some a penknife, some a flask. A gunman sticks a gun there, a reefer smoker sticks a spring knife. Most men stick a handkerchief or a bunch of keys. I'm apt to stick a billfold on my hip, myself.

I'd never stick a paid-up hotel bill there. But if St. Erme hadn't stuck his away, waiting at the President for Elinor Darrie this morning, with his name on it, and the name of his hotel on it, he might never have been identified. Or if old Adam MacComerou had not been introduced by chance to him previously by Dexter, and if old MacComerou hadn't happened to have a good memory for faces, and also if St. Erme's big floppy Panama hat hadn't fallen off his head by the time that big gray car went rushing past the place here in its mad getaway at twilight, and furthermore if St. Erme's head hadn't been rolled back on the car cushions, with his face turned up to all the light that there was in the twilight sky—giving old MacComerou a chance to recognize him— he might never have been found.

For even with the best of circumstances, old MacComerou couldn't be more than three-quarters sure, in the short time he had had to see St. Erme in passing, a man he had met but once. And he couldn't be sure of murder; he could hardly even more than guess at it, and that only because of the pale look of St. Erme's face and the look of that red-eyed little man. And it might have been hours before he or someone else might have thought it advisable, after discussing it back and forth, to notify the police. And so he might never have been found.

But he had been found.

I didn't have that envelope any more on my own hip, I realized while I was squatting there beside him. That waddy envelope which old Buchanan's housekeeper had given me, and which I had folded and stuck away when I was leaving my stalled car at the road entrance in the dusk to find a wrench.

It had probably worked out of my pocket in the car, or maybe while I had been sitting in MacComerou's living room, having coffee with the girl and Postmaster Quelch and Trooper Stone, before coming down here with Stone. I had had it last, so far as I could remember, when I had been going down the road toward Route 7 with that big yellow mongrel slavering at my wheels, just before I had met her. I might have lost it while examining the ground down there on the road edge overlooking Dead Bridegroom's Pond, of course.

All right, I might find it again, and I might not. If I found it, I would tuck it away more securely. And if I didn't find it, it was a payment for nothing that I had earned. I hadn't even opened the envelope to see how much was in it.

But I knew now, after hearing how much St. Erme had had on him, that it had been fifty fifties in that envelope of mine. As sure as hell.

Postmaster Quelch appeared to join the group around us in the headlights. I didn't think at the moment about the girl we had left with Quelch back at MacComerou's house. I didn't think about what might have happened to her, or where she might be, or with anyone or alone now, when I saw him. I was just sick, seeing what had been done to the man she had loved—that man who would never be a man again.

I just thought, *Here comes the automatic phonograph again*, when I saw Quelch, with his high-kneed strut, his tall celluloid collar and bow tie, his throat muscles already quivering to speak, coming around from back of the car and joining the group around. With Quelch to take the pulpit, I could continue with what manual examination was necessary, beneath Rosenblatt's and MacComerou's eyes, without all those questions about and-so-on.

I knew where I had been myself during that hour, and every minute of it; and if they didn't believe me it was their hard luck. Even if I had found St. Erme's right hand in my hip pocket, I would still have known.

"Postmaster Quelch from down at Whippleville," Quelch introduced himself with sprout-chested geniality to old Adam MacComerou, reaching down a hand. "Professor MacComerou, I believe? I met you when you first moved up on May twenty-seventh, about three-fifteen in the afternoon, when you stopped in at the post office in your station wagon, on your way up to open up your house, to give instructions about your mail."

"Glad to see you again, Mr. Quelch," said MacComerou, reaching around to take the proffered hand, without any particular gladness or pain. "I rather blew my head off the other day when you called me up, I think, and I may owe you an apology for it. Or was it you? I don't like to hang up so sharply, but I was busy writing, and I don't like to be summoned to the phone."

Old Adam had found a lower plate of teeth since I had first come upon him in his garden and walked back up the road with him; and he didn't mumble mushily any more. He had a rather deep, sympathetic voice, now that he had something to work his tongue against. His appearance may have been improved somewhat, too; though one row of teeth isn't much better than none so far as looks go, and his jaws were still wrinkled and flat.

But when a man is old he doesn't care for appearances. That's one thing about it.

"I know how it is, Professor," said Quelch, standing over us, and looking down with interest at St. Erme's body on the road. "I hate to be interrupted myself when I am thinking. Yes, it was me you mean, I guess. It was nine days ago I called you up, a week ago last Monday, about six-ten in the evening, right after the evening mail truck had come in with the New York mail, that had a special-delivery for you. You had given me instructions to hold your mail for you to call for—that there wouldn't be anything important, probably, and you didn't want to bother to have it delivered by the RFD man because maybe you would forget to look in your box for maybe a couple of weeks and it might spill out and get rained on, or somebody might come along and take it. And there hasn't been much of anything has come for you except scientific magazines and college catalogues, none of them very interesting or I guess important, so I have just been holding it till you got around to getting it.

"But there was this special-delivery letter for you from your lawyers, I guess they are, Barnaby and Barnaby, Counsellors at Law, Ten Wall Street, New York City, and I didn't know if you might want it delivered out to your place right away. It looked like a check in it, holding it up to the light, though I couldn't quite make out the amount. I thought you might want to know about it, anyway, which was why I ventured to disturb you. Of course when you told me not to bother you, that was all right, too."

"I'm much obliged to you," said old MacComerou. "My quarterly dividend check. I had forgotten that it was about due. I'll pick it up sometime."

"I brought it along with me," said Quelch. "I got it here, with my book. I thought I might as well earn the nine-cent delivery fee. It's a registered special, with return receipt. If you'll just sign for it."

He reached the letter, along with a dogeared memorandum book and a stub of pencil, down across MacComerou's shoulders. But old Adam was mad by that time, with his bat ears twitching and with his shrewd old blue eyes rolling sidewise in his head.

"Don't bother me about it now, you jabbering clown!" he said. "I am not going to sign for it now."

"A clabbering jown, am I?" said Mr. Quelch. "Why, you hald-beaded, hat-beard——"

He could think of the adjectives, but he couldn't pronounce them very well, with the indignation that was seething in his brain beneath his three long plastered hairs. "Bald-headed" and "bat-eared" were probably what he had meant to say. They were pretty obvious about old Adam. A man's ears that stick out stick out. But Quelch couldn't think of any noun. It's hardly an insult to call a man a psychologist. Though there are some men—like a chemistry instructor from Harvard that I had at Southern State—who think that if anyone calls them professor, it is a fighting word.

Not that they aren't full professors; they just don't like to be called that. But old Adam wasn't a man like that. He had been annoyed by Quelch's garrulity. As he had been annoyed by some of my remarks, maybe. But he had self-control.

"I am a representative of the United States government," Quelch articulated with dignity. "Appointed by the President as one of his first acts when he came into office because I am a good and loyal Democrat, and now blanketed under permanent civil service like all others, under the new law. Even a Republican President couldn't remove me. You and nobody else can talk to me like that. A clabbering—a cabbering—a jabbering jown."

"The quarterly check from Barnaby and Barnaby is for the sum of eight hundred and twenty-nine dollars and some odd cents, I believe, Mr. Quelch," said old Adam with tight-lipped courtesy. "Unless they have altered my investment portfolio to provide more profitable dividend producers, which no Wall Street trust lawyers ever do. Open the envelope yourself and see how much it is for, if you're interested."

"Why, that's nice of you, Professor," said Mr. Quelch, mollified. "It'd be against the law for me to open your registered mail for you, though, even if you wanted me to, until I'd handed it to you, and you had signed a receipt for it, and handed it back to me. I wasn't curious about how much your income is, don't misunderstand me. Every man's private business is his own. Multiplying that by four, that would be about thirty-three hundred and sixteen dollars every year, with maybe a couple of dollars over for the odd cents, depending on how odd they were. That's a right nice income. All right, I'll hold it for you as long as you want, Professor. How is your mother, by the way? Is she still with you?"

Old Adam's brown bat ears stood out on his head at the question. A wrinkle of skin seemed to creep across his pale bald skull, as if a bug were creeping along underneath his scalp. Over his shoulder he stared up at Quelch with his pale incredulous stare. He looked horrified, nothing else.

Maybe he had loved his mother. He had never loved, I think, another woman.

"In God's name, how could my mother be with me still?" he said. "She's been dead for twenty years. You never knew her, certainly. What made you ask that, Quelch?"

"Maybe it was your wife, then," said Quelch. "Or maybe it wasn't a lady, but some old man. It was raining pitchforks, and there was rain sloshing down the post office windows and down the windows of your station wagon, and I couldn't see out and in so well. I didn't notice particularly. But it was some old party with a nice pink old wrinkled smiling face and bright blue eyes, setting in the front seat beside you that you had got out of, all wrapped up in a big blankety kind of overcoat, with a shawl over their head. Come to think of it, he had a red necktie on, so he must have been a man."

"Oh," said old Adam. "That was old Squibbs you must have seen. An old faithful retainer of mine, well along in his eighties. He came up to spend the summer with me, but the somewhat primitive conditions were too much for him, and he left in less than a week.

"I live quite alone, Mr. Quelch," he added after a moment. "A retired old bachelor, with my garden and my writing and my books, except for what companionship I have had from John Flail while he worked about the place. And he was always a taciturn type of Indian. Now he's gone. I planned to get married once when I was young. But something always came up to prevent it. I never did."

"You ought to keep a cat, like me," said Mr. Quelch. "You can always talk to a cat. That was one thing I noticed about that old party, Mr. Squibbs, that was with you, that made me like him. He had a gray cat on his lap that he was talking to. But cats take milk, of course. I'm sorry that he's gone. . . ."

A man like Quelch could talk on like that, annoying a man like old MacComerou, with this thing lying here. But I was glad Quelch had the pulpit, while I looked at that trephine job again, to see what the devil had been trying to get out of that dead brain.

It was then she came. The girl who had loved St. Erme. Whom he would never marry now. She came down there on the road where we were looking at it.

Maybe worse even than finding that arm without a hand, that was the worst.

There we were, gathered in the headlights in front of the car, about the body of St. Erme which had been found. Which lay on the corduroy with its bones bludgeoned, with its face stripped and augered by those sadistic things which had been done by a depraved maniac, in its silky gabardine suit that was all muck now, and its white silk shirt that was all brown swamp water. With the love-knot cuff link at the wrist of its left hand which had lain on the seat lightly and protectively back of her where she sat at the wheel all the way up, heading for Connecticut and then Vermont upon their wedding journey; and with the link on its right wrist that had no hand now.

I hadn't thought of her. He just made me sick. And if anyone thinks it's funny for a doctor to be that way, he can try being one.

I had just completed my examination. All that could be made without an autopsy, and there would be no need of that. MacComerou had been answering Quelch over his shoulder, kneeling there across from me. Rosenblatt, with his wrinkled forehead and his cap pushed back on his bush of hair, was just squatting, watching everything my hands touched and everything I did. And those others around us in a ring, standing silently—all except Quelch —watching.

And maybe Quelch had just made some remark about how the poor fellow didn't seem quite so good-looking as he had been back at the post office, or perhaps some remark that he looked younger; and maybe old Adam had just replied that death makes all men timeless. I knew all that I would ever know about him now. I was getting up from my knees. And then I heard her.

"Inis!"

Oh, in the name of all suffering mercy, that fool Quelch had brought her along down here in his car with him!

He had probably left her in it, back along up the road with the twenty or fifty other parked cars; and maybe had patted her wrist or chucked her under the chin and told her to stay there like a good little girl. But he wasn't the sort of man that women ever listen to, though they may laugh at them or with them. She had got out and come down the road, having heard that something had been found.

"Inis! Where are you, Inis? Oh, where is he?"

Oh, in the name of suffering mercy!

She was right back of the car now, and coming around it. In her white coat, with her dark eyes staring, and her hands half feeling out before her, as if she were dazed and blind. Across from me MacComerou crouched with his mouth tight, with his shrewd eyes turned toward where she was coming, terribly pale. Even Rosenblatt looked as if he could be flattened with a breath.

Some of the gawking fools standing around us—they hadn't any better sense—were making way to let her through.

"Inis!" she cried. "I know you're here! What have they done to you? Why don't they let you answer me?"

Oh, Christ! It was the way she said it. It got you down. Calling for a man who has only a left hand. Who would never be alive any more.

MacComerou shot a tight-mouthed look at me, and I shot one to Trooper Stone, standing back of Rosenblatt, with his broad changeless smile.

"She's your baby, Stone," I said to him from the edges of my lips. "Get her out of here. Quick!" Aloud I called out,

"Is that you, Elinor? They found the car, all right, you see, as Stone told us. Look in the rear, and see if that purse there isn't yours."

I got up, and went toward her, moving in, in front of her, with Stone. We did a nice take-out, between us.

"They've found some tracks," I said. "They're all just looking at them. It still looks fairly hopeful. Of course he may have been a little hurt. But I don't think there's anything to worry about, too much."

She put her hands upon my breast, with a breathless gasp.

"Oh, Dr. Riddle! You haven't found him? You aren't trying to tell me an untruth? Please! I thought I heard someone say that they had found him! Please don't lie to me!"

"No," I said. "We haven't found him. You must have heard them talking about something else. He's probably quite all right, Elinor. Probably quite unharmed."

"Swear it!" she said.

Well, every man has his own conscience, which he must answer to at God's white judgment day.

"So help me God!" I said.

She walked back, stumbling a little, between Stone and me, then toward Stone's police car.

"I thought I heard him, Dr. Riddle!" she said. "I thought I heard him! I thought that he was there, but he wouldn't answer me! That was the most harrowing feeling of all! I'd rather know that he is dead than half alive! I really would! Hearing me, and not answering me, because something kept him from it! I don't like it down here! I don't like it! Please take me away!"

I got her into the car beside Stone, still a little on the edge of hysteria. With all that she had passed through. Perhaps I did tell her then, with a brief word, and quietly—to administer an anodyne to her uncertainty—that the man she had known as Inis St. Erme was dead, and she would see him no more.

But nothing worse than that.

I gave Stone the nod to get her away, and keep her away, with that. He reached over across her and shook my hand, for no reason, before starting back with her.

We got an army cot from John Flail's tar-paper shack, a little farther back.

Flail had lived in a pigpen there, a mess. Blankets strewn about on the floor. A coffeepot had burned dry on the wood range, whose embers had gone out, though it was still warm. A plate with cold fried eggs and cold potatoes on the table. Two chairs with broken backs, one of which had been overset.

There was the cot on which John Flail's body had been laid, beneath a sheet. I didn't want to look at it. There was another cot, and the troopers took that, and took it on down and put that poor thing on it, and brought it back up, and put it in Flail's shack there, with a sheet over it, too. I don't think that it minded being left there, with that other black Indian-eyed man, John.

St. Erme had been found. He had to be, to make the terror real. But that was not all of it. His right hand had not been found. Corkscrew, also, had not been found.

It would seem that it would take no time at all to find him. With the hundred or more men who were already there. Men who knew all the countryside. With their lanterns and their guns. With him on foot, with his sawed-off legs. With his face—torn ear, cat teeth, red eyes, matted hair, and all of it. In his extraordinary clothing still, all except that damned saw-tooth hat. For if he had discarded his clothing—his glaring black and white checked sport coat, his green shirt, his gaudy tie—it would somewhere be found, like his hat. And even if he had hidden it, he would have been no less conspicuous, naked. But he was not found.

I have gone all over it in my own mind. I know the look of him better than I know my own face. The way he pinched his ear. The way he smiled. The way he held that dead and mangled kitten. The quiet voice in which he spoke his Latin.

Suns may rise and sink again. But for us, when our brief light goes out, there is one eternal night for sleeping.

Sleeping. . . .

How much he knew, that little man! Only a tramp, but more than he seemed. As are all men, no doubt. All men born beneath God. And, not less, those given over to the devil.

I know him well. He is near to me right now—Corkscrew, old Doc. Very near and very quiet, and lying hidden.

I know that he is near, although I cannot see him. Perhaps within ten feet of me.

I will see him, I know that, before this night is ended.

I do not want to see him, but I must. It is not for a man to choose. God made me be a doctor.

Lying very quiet—old Doc, old Corkscrew. Yet I must awake him, I must see him. And, before I see him, in the shape he appeared to Elinor and St. Erme upon the road, I will see that damned killer in his own shape, I think.

MacComerou had got close to him, somehow. He had got very close, had old Adam, with his shrewd old brain. With his shrewd old brain that knew too much of murder.

I can see the dark night down there in the swamp, and the torches moving here and there, far off. I can hear the voices of the men calling to each other. Old Adam and Gregori Unistaire and I had stayed behind. We were going through the huge sawdust heaps, those damp mountainous piles of soft-footed rotted lignin, which had been down in the old ravine back of the sawmill for a hundred years, from the time when all this country had been much more populated than it is now. The old sawdust of a hundred years, consumed by a slow cold fireless burning, piled down on the slope of the ravine.

Old Adam and Gregori and I were going through them, plowing through them to our knees, wading around and up and down the slope along the edge of the ravine. With our flashes, with clubs in our fists. For Gregori had had a surrealistic idea that Corkscrew might be hiding down there, and Old Adam hadn't wanted him to look alone.

And there was an imminence of sliding in the soft stuff all beneath us. As we plowed, we had got farther apart, pausing and turning aside to look at some hillock stirring, and so widening our distance a little more, before we might be aware of it. Along the sloping side of the ravine back of the old sawmill.

And then MacComerou's light, where he was, had gone out. I saw it go out, though Gregori didn't.

"MacComerou!" I shouted. "Adam!"

But there was no answer from him. I stood knee-deep in the damp heaps of pith, with my cudgel in my fist. I put out my own torch, too, and moved aside. The seconds seemed like hours. There was someone creeping through that sawdust with a knife.

"Adam!" I called. "Damn you, old Adam!"

"What ees it, Harry, my friend!" Unistaire called out to me. "Where are you?"

His light had moved halfway down the sawdust slopes toward the bottom of the ravine, where MacComerou's light had gone out.

"Watch out, Gregori!" I called to him. "Watch out! Put out your torch! The Professor's has gone out! Adam! Where are you, old Adam?"

"Harry!" Unistaire screamed to me, still with his light

on. "Here is something! It is a body! Here! Come down and help me! It is buried in the sawdust heaps, with sawdust in its mouth and eyes!"

I plowed toward his light, which was focused downward. Moving quietly, straining my eyes through the darkness around me.

"Who?" I called. "Not Quelch's? Not Rosenblatt's?"

"No, Harry! A bald white-fringed head! An old man, Harry! The sawdust sticks so. Oh, my God, it is the old man himself! It is old MacComerou! Harry! Harry!"

His light came floundering and plowing up toward me, waving from side to side. I heard his sobbing breath, as I plunged down to meet him, with my darkened torch clubbed in my fist.

"Watch out!" I called with a dry breathless throat. "Watch out for your light!"

"Harry! He's dead and buried, back down there! Har——"

Unistaire's light went out, within twenty feet of me. There was only the blackness, and the sliding underfoot.

I turned on my torch, sweeping it around me. The damp sawdust heaps were starting to flow downward. They were moving downward in a great soft sea. Unistaire lay ten feet from me, already partly buried, with his feet upward on the sliding slope, his head down. With a great red gash across where his throat had been, as wide as the mouth of a tiger laughing.

I got to him, sweeping my light around. The blood was

still pouring from his throat. His eyes were on me. But his life was ended.

I wheeled the flash around me, crouching.

"All right!" I said. "All right! I'm here! I'm watching. I'm no surrealist! Try that on me, damn you!"

Why he didn't, I don't know. Perhaps he was caught to the thighs himself in the sliding stuff, and couldn't move fast enough. Fast enough to come in at me, or to get away, if his strike missed. Perhaps he was struggling to get out of it in this moment for his own dear life. Perhaps he would never choose a moment when he knew that I was watching.

I snapped out my torch. I got Unistaire's body by the feet. I dragged him backward up the sliding avalanche, plunging and plowing, with that soft stuff sliding away beneath me and all around. I got him clear out onto solid ground, as the whole top of the slope caved away, and went cascading down.

And I was shouting. . . .

There is a gang of men digging now with shovels. But old MacComerou's body, down there toward the bottom of the ravine, may have already begun to sink down deeper of its own weight, after the sawdust was disturbed by Unistaire, uncovering him. It was certainly buried far deeper under those scores of tons of damp rotted lignin refuse that slid down.

Deep, deep, old Adam MacComerou lies, with his great brain, with the sawdust in his eyes.

It will be like thimbling out a lake, to move all that stuff with shovels. Nor was I able to put my finger precisely on the spot where Unistaire's light had been focused—the spot where he had stumbled on him—when he began to scoop and brush away the damp sawdust from old Adam's face, shouting out in terror to me. At the best, with all men digging, it must take many days.

It was after they had found me there with Unistaire's body at the edge of the sawdust pit, when they had come running in answer to my shout, that the troopers told me Lieutenant Rosenblatt wanted me to return to MacComerou's house. Rosenblatt wanted to be able to keep an eye on me, it seemed, while the search went on.

And I am here.

It was more than an hour ago that Rosenblatt went surging out, with his wrinkled angry pugdog face, with a shout to Trooper Stone, at that scream which sounded like Quelch's, down toward John Flail's.

Rosenblatt went crashing through the screen door and plunging down off the porch, and running up the drive past the barn, up past the water tank on the stony pasture slope, toward the path that cuts through the woods in back, over toward the swamp and John Flail's.

It is shorter that way, much shorter, to get to the swamp and John Flail's. Not half the distance as by the road in front up to the Swamp Road, then off and down it. If John Flail had taken that way home last evening from MacComerou's here, just before that gray car came rushing up the road, he would probably be alive now. But he always went the road way, for fear of ghosts. So he is one himself now.

Rosenblatt thought that Stone was in the bedroom just beyond the door, getting a brief, light hour of sleep—after the night before, which Stone had spent up on duty—when he went rushing out. He thought that Stone was in there, and so did I.

"Take care of her, Ed!" Rosenblatt shouted as he went slamming out. "This time I'm going to run that bastard down!"

A man like Stone—a man like Stone who is a trained policeman—would have come out of that closed bedroom door within half a minute, at Rosenblatt's parting shout, I should have known. Out of any sleep, he would have waked up instantly to take over, reaching for his gun, without bothering to put his shoes on, if he had removed them, and would have come out.

At once. To protect that sleeping girl. To be the guardian dog, to arrange the defenses, to say what lamps should be left burning and what put out. He would have had some strategical plan with which to meet the killer if he came. He would have had his gun. And there would have been two of us. It may well take two men to handle that devil. He has a knife, and he's strong.

It was Rosenblatt's fault for thinking he was leaving Stone to take over. It was mine for not shouting to him immediately to come back, when Stone did not appear.

I waited for Stone to emerge from the bedroom, sitting at old Adam MacComerou's desk here, getting the terms of the problem arranged in my mind, and beginning to make my notes. Thinking that I heard Stone moving around in there, just beyond the door. Thinking that Stone had found a lamp in there and lit it, and was perhaps fussing with his necktie and combing his hair, and would be out at any moment.

I waited ten minutes, I waited twenty, working on my notes. I waited sixty seconds more, with my pencil motionless. Then I knew Stone wasn't in there. It was something of a shock to realize it.

I called to him quietly, "Stone!" So as not to awake and frighten her. But I knew he wasn't there. I went to the door, with club in hand. I braced myself, and opened it. But there was no one there.

An open window, with the screen removed. The bed was empty. With the door wide open from the living room behind me, letting in all the light of the white lamp that could shine in, I entered, step by step. Watching from the edges of my eyes, half turning to right and left, quickly, letting no shadow get behind me. I closed and locked the window. Then I came out again.

The way Stone had been got rid of is obvious. A tap at the window beside his bed. He awakes instantly. To see a face that he knows, that is not the face of Corkscrew, that is not the face of death, as he knows it and is looking for it. The face of a man who is helping to pursue the search for the red-eyed little killer, and perhaps is helping to direct it. Not the killer at all. It would never occur to him. A man who during the murder hour was somewhere else. A man who was alibied.

Stone! This is me! Lieutenant Rosenblatt out in the living room wanted me to tell you, without letting Miss Darrie know! They have found St. Erme's hand down by Dead Bridegroom's Pond, around on the other side of the pond, back somewhere in the woods! Lieutenant Rosenblatt wants you to go down there and take charge, without letting her know, while he stays here with her! Quietly!

Or: Lieutenant Rosenblatt wants you to go get St. Erme's hat, Trooper Stone, and go around unobtrusively with it among all the searchers, finding out how many heads it will fit on, without letting Miss Darrie know. Or: Lieutenant Rosenblatt wants you to go down to the next place that has a phone, without letting Miss Darrie know, and phone the police in Spardersburg, Pennsylvania, to find out what they may know about a man named Gus who used to work in a lunch wagon, and to stay there till you have got some positive information.

Or anything else nonsensical but that might sound plausible, that will keep Stone away for a long time. Lieutenant Rosenblatt is staying on guard himself. And Stone goes off on a wild-goose chase.

Or perhaps, as Stone removed the screen and slid his legs out over the window ledge, with both hands on the ledge to ease himself down, with his gun holstered, with that known face waiting out in the night for him, he was killed with the knife right there.

Stone was not here, as Rosenblatt thought, that is all. After Stone, he got Rosenblatt out on a wild-goose chase himself.

There is no gun or weapon of any kind in the house. There is no bread knife with a serrated blade in the kitchen, such as he has himself. There is no knife of any sort. Even the stove poker out there has been removed. There are no heavy objects such as doorstops. It is almost as if the house had been deliberately and carefully denuded, at some time in the past, of all small common objects of assault which a maniac might use. Of course, he may have done it himself during tonight. There is nothing heavier than the books on the bookshelf above me—*Who's Who,* and old MacComerou's own massive buckram tome that has in it all there is to be known of murder. But I couldn't hit him with that and make it hurt.

I went out a while ago to get the crank from the old Draco coupe on the drive near the back porch, but it had been taken. My surgical instruments—not that any of them would be of much use—were taken from the unlocked trunk compartment at some moment tonight. Before I had met her, even. I found them missing down there at Dead Bridegroom's Pond, which was why I locked the car when I came back.

I haven't dared to go out farther into the night, in search of any weapons. Out to the barn, or even so far as the garden.

I daren't leave her alone here. Nor am I sure that I should be able to see him first, or soon enough, out in the darkness. I have good eyes, perfect emmetropic eyes. But his eyes are no less good. And perhaps in the night they are a cat's eyes, not quite human.

The door into the little front hallway, at the other end of the room behind me, is locked with a key, and the front door itself is nailed and padlocked. The window in the bedroom is closed and locked. The copper screen at the window beside me, against which the moths are fluttering with their crimson eyes and white dusty bodies, cannot be pushed in. I have planted a chair with a lot of pans balanced on it against the planked door out in the kitchen that opens out into the woodshed in the back. I have done the same against the kitchen screen door.

There is the white gasoline lamp here in the living room on the desk, which illuminates the whole room fairly. There is a yellow kerosene lamp burning on the shelf out in the kitchen above the sink. There are no other lamps with fuel in them. The fuel would be out in the barn, perhaps.

The telephone bell at times still gives forth its ghostly jangle. But there is no meaning in it. The wire has been cut.

I broke up one of the kitchen chairs and took a leg of it. I have it across my knees. It is not very heavy. It would be only a deflecting weapon against that knife. But a man likes to have something in his fist.

He might stand out there in the night, of course, and shoot me. I have thought of that, weighing the hazards of it against the hazards of keeping constantly alert in perfect darkness in this creaky house, trying to keep him from the girl that I could no longer see, with him perhaps having cat's eyes.

I do not think he has a gun. Guns make a noise. Gun bullets have their own rifling prints; and guns can be traced. The firing of a gun leaves powder flecks that can be determined on a man's hand or wrist.

No, he is strong, and he has always trusted to his own hands. He would like to do the thing in darkness and silence. Doing murder with a common weapon that cannot be traced when found—a stone picked up by the roadside, or something like that—has always been his specialty.

Though he bought that serrated knife himself in Danbury, for a dollar and fifteen cents. With the girl that he was going to kill right there beside him, God help her.

I have got all the facts down.

That is it.

Bright blazing intuitions may go rushing through a man's mind, swifter and more terrible than lightning, flashing over a landscape that seems clear in every detail. Then they go out, and there is only a greater blackness.

They cannot be trusted. A dozen times tonight I have had the flashing thought that old Adam MacComerou himself, with his big brown bat ears, his pale wrinkled eyes and mushy talk, with his smooth old muscles sliding beneath his

pale skin like the muscles of a tiger, with his big old brain
that knew too much of murder, was trying to kill me. After
he had seen my car parked down there right at the entrance
to the Swamp Road, as I had said it was, and I had handed
him back his little wrench, with him saying to me mushily,
"Perhaps I had better give it to you!" and the owl howling.
And a few steps later, turning with that crank in my hand
that I had picked up, which had struck the rattlesnake the
mortal blow in its blind heave—though I hadn't known it at
the time—and seeing him right there behind me, with that
big rock in his fist. And for a long second, it had seemed to
me, he held the rock, while I held the crank, before he had
tossed it over into the weeds.

I had laid the crank across my knees and kept my right
hand half on it, all the way back down to his place here.

Yes, I had had a blind flashing intuition that he would
like to kill me, when I first came on him in his garden, for
no reason. And more than once again tonight. Down there
in the huge sloping sawdust heaps, when his light had gone
quietly out, most of all. Before Unistaire had found his old
body.

Old Adam MacComerou, who wrote *Homicidal Psychopathology*, that profound and lucid analysis of the murderous
mind. Perhaps some way he had gone crazy, I thought. One
of the most brilliant men that science has produced. Though
it had been impossible that a clear mind like that could ever
go crazy. And I knew that he lived here quietly at his place

all the time, a little gruff over the telephone, and not very neighborly, but interested in his garden and his books. A perfectly sane life.

Blinding lightning flashes. But no good. Here are the facts. I have sweated to get them down. Every one of them, omitting nothing, however trivial it might be, or might seem to be. And there is one perfect criminal, and one only, through all of it. He is right there, right through it. He is there from the beginning. He is St. Erme. He is that man who called himself S. Inis St. Erme, though his name may have been John Jones or Judkiss Smith.

From the beginning, from his first appearance, St. Erme is the complete and perfect criminal. And no one else.

That insurance business between him and Dexter stank. Dexter, a small businessman, hard-pressed for cash, may have been only a stooge for him. Dexter doesn't seem very bright. He may not have realized the criminality. St. Erme, having discovered him, goes to him with a proposition for an insurance fraud. St. Erme will insure his life in Dexter's favor, then pretend to kill himself, and let Dexter collect. Maybe letting Dexter keep ten or twenty per cent of the proceeds for his trouble.

St. Erme comes into an insurance agency which he has picked. A reputable firm, but owned by an old man, and doing only a modest little business, both of which items may indicate him as a man not too sharp and bright—old Cousin Paul Riddle is a lot older than my father, and I never heard in any family talk that he was ever a ball of fire. Having an old, old examining doctor, too. Though St. Erme was strong enough. He was—he is—as strong as hell, with nothing wrong with him. So perhaps the age of the doctor didn't make any difference.

In the office he meets this shy and pretty little girl, without friends or family. He knows that no man has ever made love to her before. It is something which any man can tell about a girl. He makes eyes at her, maybe taking her out to lunch that day. He gets to know her, so that he will seem to have more substance and more background as an insurable prospect, by using her.

Who is this young man St. Erme, anyway, Miss Darrie, who had applied for twenty-five thousand dollars' insurance, with double indemnity in case of accidental death? I rather understood from some remark he made that you know him?

Why, I don't really know him, Mr. Riddle. But he's the son of an oil man from Oklahoma, I think, who left him a lot of money, though he doesn't like to talk about it. His mother is a Scots-Indian. He's an investor, I think. He makes money on the stock exchange whenever there is an opportunity, too, and is interested in a lot of different businesses. One of the small things that he is interested in as a side venture is an inventing business run by a garage man named Mr. Dexter. Mr. Dexter has a lot of inventions—I don't understand all the technical details about them—but Mr. St. Erme thinks that some of them may be worth millions when they are finished. Of course he doesn't know. He invests in a lot of things that way, I think.

Yes, he told me about his relations with Dexter, Miss Darrie. He has named Dexter as his beneficiary. That is what he wanted to get the insurance for specifically, to give Dexter protection and a sense of stability, without tying up his own money in cash. It was what his lawyers had advised him—I'm not sure if he mentioned their name to me. Dexter's credit rating is pretty bad. Still, it is St. Erme we are insuring and not Dexter. I'm glad to have more details on him. You say you knew his mother?

Oh, no, sir. I never actually knew her. She lived out in Oklahoma. She is dead. I just said she was a Scots-Indian.

Yes, I noticed how black his eyes are. Probably got 'em from her. Thank you for the information on him, Miss Darrie. You aren't sweet on him, are you?

Oh, no, sir. Nothing like that. You are always teasing me. Why, he's old. I mean, he's thirty-three. Of course, I don't mean that's really old, Mr. Riddle. Why, look at you, you're seventy-nine, and look how young you are. Still, he seems sort of old to me. He's just taken me out to dinner once or twice. . . .

And so, through her, he is Inis St. Erme, the rich man's son from somewhere out in Oklahoma; and he has got his insurance. All that he needs to do now is to kill himself, let Dexter collect like a good stooge, and give Dexter his ten or twenty per cent.

He has got it all figured out, how he will be killed. He will be riding in Dexter's car, a conspicuous car. He will pick up some tramp, the worse-looking the better. He'll show himself to different people with the tramp. Then, in some lonely setting, he'll kill the tramp, change clothes with him, and in a dusky twilight setting stage a scene of rushing terror, in which he will be the tramp, hunched over the wheel, making faces, blaring his horn, while the tramp, in his own clothes, sits sprawled in the car seat beside him, with his own coat on and his own fine Panama hat down over his face—looking pretty dead, because he is. He will rush away to nowhere.

The next morning, or a day or two later, maybe, the police will find the car parked on the outskirts of some small city, with blood on it. They will check the license, and inquire about it from its owner. Dexter will tell them, as St. Erme has instructed him to, that he lent it to St. Erme, and that he hasn't heard from St. Erme, and had been getting a little worried.

The police will back-track on the car. It was so conspicuous that someone must have seen it and St. Erme in it. They will learn about the tramp who had been with him, and that rushing scene of terror. They will track back and find how St. Erme had picked up the tramp along the road. They won't be able to trace the tramp back, because tramps don't have any background. They won't be able to trace him forward, because he is dead, and buried in some lonely ravine.

St. Erme is missing, with all the indications of murder, in what is a not uncommon type of crime. After a time Dexter, according to St. Erme's instructions, will identify some body that has been found after being in some river a long time, and the insurance will be paid to Dexter.

It fits, in every detail of St. Erme's actions. A fairly crude play, with Dexter as the stooge in the background, and at the cost of killing a worthless little tramp, which Dexter does not have to be told about. But cruder plays have been gotten away with by brighter men. Insurance companies can be defrauded. In case of established death, they pay.

Poor little Corkscrew, standing by the roadside with his dead mangled kitten that he felt so sorry for! Liking to ride in Cadillacs. Poor old Corkscrew, poor old Doc.

But why, in God's name, the girl? Why the girl here, with her lovely face and her clear innocent trusting young heart? After he had played up to her to establish himself with the Riddle agency as a solid and reputable person, why didn't he just drop her?

She had served his purpose. He was not a man to love. It sticks out all over him. Even she herself, ignorant as she was of men, had known by instinct that he did not care for women. The whole thing of love bored him, and women bored him.

So why keep it up?

He had learned from her that she had a little money of her own, that was why. She had a few dollars more than twenty-five hundred in the bank, the proceeds of the sale of her grandmother's house. That was only a fraction as much as he would get from the insurance. But if he could get his hands on it, it would be so much extra, and it would be sure, at least. He was a businessman, as he had told her. He liked to stick his fingers in a lot of pies.

He can't just borrow the money from her, though. That would break down his whole character as a rich man, and spoil his other game. He can't use the wiretapping scheme or the gilt-edged-stock scheme. What he plans is to go into the bank with her some time when she is drawing a little check for herself.

He has learned that, in making out a check, she always writes the day first, and then her signature, and pauses then to debate with herself whether she will make the amount five dollars or seven-fifty. In the bank with her—which he has pretended to her is his own bank, too—he will get her to start making out a check for twenty or twenty-five dollars, while he pretends to be making out one of his own beside her. Then, just at the moment when she had written in the word for the amount, and before she has drawn the line or put down the # to terminate it, he will distract her attention, and give her some reason why he is taking her check to cash with his own mythical one.

In the way he did it, he seized her arm and called attention to their car out in front, with some hocus-pocus about some suspicious-looking man who had been staring at it. He asked her to watch it, while at some other counter he wrote "Five Hundred" after the word "Twenty," and put the number $2500 down, and went back to the window to cash it.

He went to a teller who, he knew, knew her by sight.

When the teller was dubious about it—a check made out to cash, in a sum practically wiping out her account—he probably explained easily that Miss Darrie was buying a house or making some investment, and said with a nod, "There is Miss Darrie now."

And she had smiled at his nod and come on back, vouching for him by her presence. Sawyer had started paying out the money, and had made some remark to her that he hoped she would profit from her investment.

Outside the bank, St. Erme had given her one of the bills, to show how rich and generous he was, telling her that he had torn up her own check, and that her money wasn't good any more. It wasn't. But he hadn't expected her to keep that bill long. Not he. For she couldn't be allowed to live now, and spoil his other game about the insurance. He will just kill her, and hide her body.

A girl without a family, without friends. No one will ever look for her. No one will ever know.

He had been cultivating her, since he had met her, with an occasional dinner or movie, with nickel trips to Staten Island and free visits to the zoo. To get her in the mood, though, for that final act—where she would go away with him where he could kill her—he had to spring marriage on her, rushing her off her feet, giving her no time to think.

Suddenly, after one special lunch that he had treated her to, saying to her, *Let's get married! Let's get married now! Let's go down right now to City Hall and get married this afternoon!*

Of course he had known that it couldn't be done. Still, the idea had excited her, as it would any girl, unless she loathed a man. Then, after he had rushed her down, and it couldn't be done, he had said to her, still keeping up the excitement, the sense of urgency, *Let's go to Connecticut! Let's drive, and make a honeymoon of it!*

It is too late to go that day, she knows. But he gets her to agree to go in the morning, and calls up Dexter from a phone booth and arranges for Dexter's car, not telling Dexter what he wanted it for, not telling Dexter about the girl, not telling Dexter it was murder. Dexter sends around the car to her, having got her address right, though not her name, and she picks him up. He stages, then, the scene that he has planned at the bank, and has her money. Now for the wedding and the honeymoon.

They get to Danbury late, as he had arranged it. But they can't be married there. *All right, let's go on up to Vermont! Come on! We've come this far! Why hesitate now? It would spoil it to turn back. Listen, if you're worried, sweet, I just thought of old John R. Buchanan, the rich man—you've heard of him, everyone has heard of him. He has his summer place up in Vermont. Maybe you've heard of it, too. Old John will give us a wonderful wedding. He's even got a wonderful honeymoon place up in the hills that he has promised to lend me. We'll head for his place, not bothering with hotels—I don't like registering in them, either. We'll get some supplies and have a picnic on the way!*

If he had said to her at the beginning, back in New York, "Let's go up to Vermont to be married," it would have seemed to her too far. They could wait three days in New York. He had to lure her on by stages, in a spirit of whipped-up excitement. To the place where he had wanted her. To some deep black lake up in some lonely district, where he could sink her body so deep with stones that it would never be found.

Dead Bridegroom's Pond. The name had frightened her when Postmaster Quelch had mentioned it. But no doubt he had thought it funny.

How could he do it to her? With her beautiful face, with her sweet and trusting young heart? A man not human. A man with no heart at all. The mother who had borne him must have been cursed and damned.

Maybe he had done it to other girls before her. That ring he gave her that doesn't fit her. Who knows? Or will ever know?

There had been that moment in Danbury when she had almost pulled back. She had felt that dark shadow. She had been afraid of him, though she didn't know what her feeling was. Perhaps she had been terrified of him all along, deep underneath, with all the deepest instincts of her life. So he had dragged the name of old John R. Buchanan out of his memory as a bait. And they had bought groceries and the picnic plates in the ten-cent store, and he had bought the knife.

And she went on with him, to what he had planned would be her death alone.

Just outside of Danbury there had been the little tramp

by the roadside, though. Maybe St. Erme had planned his own death to be a little later. Maybe not until one more insurance premium had been paid. But that little tramp, with his repulsive face, with his extraordinary and unforgettable clothing, was too marvelous to pass over. He presented the opportunity to St. Erme to kill two birds with one stone. Or knife.

Poor damned little Corkscrew! Poor old Doc, with his quiet voice and his sorrow over a dead kitten and his little courteous nice manners and his Latin. Where he came from, who will ever know? I wonder if he really ever was a doctor? It is not education only that keeps a man from going down.

Not education, but something hard inside him. Something that says, *I'll face the issue. It's my hat, all right. It was probably my own stolen surgical instruments that were used. The fifty fifty-dollar bills that have been found in a white envelope marked "For Dr. Riddle" in the blood down on the road edge overlooking Dead Bridegroom's Pond are doubtless mine, lost out of my pocket. But that car did not pass me, I'll stand on that. I never saw it. I'll stick to that.*

He took her down there by the black lake to kill her, leaving that little tramp in the car to be killed after he had come back up, when he would change clothes with him, and drive on. He stooped by the lake shore to pick up a rock and kill her. In the twilight, by the deep black waters. And she screamed. She screamed, "Don't!"

He thought she had guessed. He caught sight of that face peering over the rock edge above. The little tramp had suspected something, too. He had followed them down.

He must be disposed of. He was dangerous. He was a witness. In a rage St. Erme went rushing after him to get him, leaving her to be disposed of when he got back.

He caught Corkscrew by the ear, and killed him there, with that scream which she had heard as she hurried up after. He changed clothes and hats swiftly, before anyone might come along the road in the twilight. From this moment onward anyone must see dirty ragged old Checked Coat, Sawtooth Blue Hat, alive, and see fine silky Gabardine Coat, Panama Hat, dead. The little tramp's shoulders were broad, for all his truncated stature, and their coats fitted. The blue saw-tooth hat, a seven and three-eighths, was even a little too big for St. Erme, but all the better, pulling down to cover more of his face. He jammed his Panama down on Corkscrew's head, with brim turned down. If it was tight, Corkscrew did not complain.

He must have made the change in half a minute. Then he went rushing back down to find her and kill her. But she was terrified, and she had hid.

Through the twilight woods, crouching, stalking her, calling her with obscenities, he had crept, with the knife in his hand. Finding her coat that she had abandoned. While she crept from him, and lay hidden with a beating heart.

She had not recognized his voice, though, using oaths that he had never used before. She had thought it was Corkscrew trying to imitate him. Perhaps, in changing into

Corkscrew's hat and coat, he had done something to change his voice, too. I must think about that.

She did not recognize him, anyway. With her myopia, she had not seen his features beneath the saw-brimmed hat, in the old coat. She had even thought his eyes looked icy pale. It was the tramp, she had thought. She could not think otherwise.

The hour was growing late for his getaway. He must not be seen too much as he raced away along the road, yet he must be seen. He had to do it before dark came completely. He could not find her, so he gave up the hunt. Perhaps she had fainted down there by the lake shore, and had fallen into the water and drowned. Perhaps she had fled so far and deep into the woods that she would never find her way out again. Perhaps she would be bitten by a rattler.

He had to give it up, anyway, to go on with his other plan. If she appeared, with a story that he had tried to kill her, it could be put down as hysteria. He would be dead then, anyway. He would show everyone that he was dead.

And so, that rushing scene of terror. A weird horn howling, a hunched driver with a grimacing face and a jeering laugh, in a checked coat and saw-tooth hat, with a finely dressed man in a Panama sprawled beside him at the wheel. A dead dog, some smashed surrealistic pictures, a jeering laugh and a squawk of his horn as he rushed past old Mac-Comerou's here, frightening MacComerou, too, like all the rest, and after that a man shambling down the road ahead, John Flail, whom he strikes and kills—knocking off, it would seem, his blue saw-tooth hat—and then on. He will dispose of the tramp's body when there are no more places to pass, and dispose of that checked coat. He will leave the car on the outskirts of a town someplace within the next fifty miles, to be found after a few days. And after a month or two, his body.

Only he turned off down the Swamp Road by mistake, not knowing the country, it would seem, and got cornered. There had to be a body of murdered St. Erme now. Within a comparatively narrow radius. If there was no body, St. Erme was not really dead.

He found that body somewhere. There was someone that he killed, besides John Flail. There was some reason that he had to cut off that right hand.

What did he do with Corkscrew's body?

Where did he get that black-eyed brown-faced body in the swamp, with its mutilated face?

Where is he now, himself?

And why in God's name didn't I see him passing me while I was there at the Swamp Road? He didn't go by me, that is all. He struck John Flail, and dropped the hat, to show that Corkscrew had gone by, that it was Corkscrew who had done it, and then he vanished. If he had gone a little farther on, only a little farther on, he would have seen me parked there by the Swamp Road.

What does he look like—Inis St. Erme of Oklahoma? Black hair, black eyes, a brown face, well dressed, about six feet tall. Most men are brown-faced in the summertime, if they are exposed to the sun at all. One out of four men, it may be, is black-haired. He may be, now, either well or poorly dressed. There are a dozen men I have seen tonight who are six feet tall, including Stone and Quelch. Only Rosenblatt and I are definitely shorter.

The black eyes, only, are a particularly distinctive feature. He had extraordinarily black eyes. Even old Paul Riddle noticed them. Black eyes, and a little blind, so that he stumbled over small unexpected obstacles. There is no such thing as black eyes, of course. It is only a phrase for dark brown eyes. Eyes are of various shades of blue and brown, with greenish mixtures of both in between. No man can have black eyes. But he can wear contact lenses of black glass.

His eyes were some other color than black, that is all which that feature tells about him. And with the black glass off, they may be cat's eyes in the dark. . . .

He didn't do a very good job with my surgical instruments in mutilating the face of that body which he planted for his own. Nor with the sawing off of the hand. Not a job that any medical man, or that old Adam MacComerou himself, with his knowledge of anatomy, would have been very proud of. He didn't do so good a job in my own particular field as I did in a garage man's field with the old Draco, when I looked at its engine and figured out the way it was put together, and how it should be taken apart. As a doctor, I may be only a fair garage man. But as a garage man, he—

Why did I put down that word?

Why did I start to assume that he might be a garage man?

The phone bell out in the kitchen gave its ghostly jangle again. Dexter, the garage man who owns the murder car, A. M. Dexter of Dexter's Day and Nite Garage on West Fourteenth Street, is a hundred miles away down in New York. When I first came here, old MacComerou called Dexter up, to ask him about his car; and that proved that.

Yet the shadow of that garage man remains sinister. With his dry metallic voice.

Yes, sinister!

Inis St. Erme—

S. Inis St. Erme, with a first name not defined.

S-I-N-I-S-S-T-E-R-M-E.

SINISTER ME! With only one S too many. Perhaps he was always a poor speller.

A man always kept a part of his own name when using an alias, I should have remembered. *Sinister*—left. *Dexter*—right. And I thought that I knew some Latin!

St. Erme—Sinister Me—was—he is—the garage man, A. M. Dexter.

I knew he had a right hand somewhere! I knew it.

What is his real appearance? A bald-headed, middle-aged man—that's Dexter, that's St. Erme, that's the murderer.

Twice as big and twice as homely as he himself was, Gus,

the day attendant whom Elinor had seen at his garage in the morning, had said, when she drove the colored boy back there, and asked if Mr. Dexter would like to check her driving—not knowing that her dazzling Inis St. Erme was Dexter, waiting at the hotel for her where he had taken a room to give himself an address for insurance.

A big powerful man, bald-headed. With eyes of some other color than black. Anyone can buy himself a wig. As Quelch said, they make them good enough to fool a barber.

Anyone with bat ears can glue them back, too, with any of various preparations, and make them seem inconspicuous with a wig of dark hair worn long—the ears, which are one of the most characteristic features of a face.

A. M. Dexter. What do the initials stand for—for what first and middle name?

Suppose I went to that phone out in the kitchen now, and rang the crank, asking for toll operator; and asked her for Mordaunt 2-8385. And suppose Mordaunt 2-8385 answered, "Dexter speaking!" And suppose I said, "This is Professor MacComerou, calling from my place up in the Berkshires." And suppose it said, "What do you want to know, Professor?"

In its dry metallic voice. While I looked through a black book, with a watch having a large second hand before me.

Or suppose, after it said, "Dexter speaking!" I just said nothing for two seconds, or said, "How are the oats growing in Times Square?" or said "Tra-la-la!" And suppose, all the same, at the end of two seconds it said, "What do you want to know, Professor?"

Yes, Professor, what did you want to know?

And suppose there are other numbers to call up, that have a different sequence of answers, for other circumstances. Dexter is down in New York. He's always there. He wouldn't come up to the country for twenty-five hundred dollars.

And suppose there is some device at the phone here, too—some device like a dictating machine, with wires and batteries—and the receiver is left off the hook. And suppose that, whenever the phone rings five long, five short, this machine speaks into the transmitter, after a few seconds, saying: "This is Professor MacComerou! Don't bother me, confound it! I don't want to be bothered! I don't want to be bothered about anything! I am busy writing!"

I can't call up. The phone line has been cut.

But suppose that that A. M. Dexter stands for Adam MacComerou Dexter?

It has been here before my eyes all along. I must get it down on paper, and slip it beneath the blotter of the desk where it may be found later, before he comes.

It is here before me, all of it.

The case-study jotting of a murderer which the old man had made a note of, at some previous time, in his spidery, shaky old hand:

The case of A, of good family, well educated, colossally conceited of own mental powers, who at age 45, unsuccessful in all undertakings and greedy for money, plots uncle's death so as to inherit modest fortune—

What "A" had the old man in mind? He never wrote a case history that he did not know intimately. He always used the right initials. That "A" must have stood for a nephew of his own—for one named Adam after him.

The notes here on the pad on the desk:

Call Barnaby & Barnaby GU 9-6400 after lunch
Inquire about mail
Have John Flail clear out cesspool & prune privet, after painting house & barn
Sugar, matches, potatoes, oranges, bacon, strawberries, bread

Call up after what lunch? How long ago? On May 28 or 29, perhaps, after he had been here only a few days, with the murderous nephew who had driven him up. Call up about changing a will, perhaps.

That old man with the bright blue eyes and the rosy withered cheeks whom Quelch had seen sitting in the station wagon, on that day Professor MacComerou first arrived, to occupy the summer place he had bought! The old, old man who had remained in it, with his shivery old bones wrapped up in greatcoat and shawl in the rainy weather, while his bald bat-eared nephew got out, and went into the post office, introducing himself as Professor MacComerou, and giving instructions for his mail to be held for call! No wonder! He didn't want the RFD man to notice an overflowing mailbox, and perhaps to stop in to inquire.

John Flail went on and painted the house and barn. No doubt he cleaned out the cesspool. He never got around to trimming the privet—perhaps the instruction was never given to him, by that bat-eared man who said he was Professor MacComerou, and who perhaps explained the old man with him as a senile old man given to delusions. John Flail was stolid, he was an Indian, he was taciturn. Probably he never came into the house at all, for fear of Ridder ghosts.

And so the old man sat here at his desk, in this house with his murderous nephew, who had assumed his identity, with no one to help him, with no one on whom he could call. Perhaps he had thought that the murderous plans in his nephew's mind were something that would never come to fruition. That he could talk him out of. But he must have known his death was on him at the last. He hid the doorstops, and all of that.

That doesn't help me. Perhaps he is sorry for it. I have the feeling that he has been trying to help me now. But he is beyond life, he is beyond the murderer's reach now himself, old Adam MacComerou.

There must have been something on his body, when Unistaire found it buried down there in the sawdust heaps, which told Unistaire who he was. Or perhaps poor Unistaire just jumped to the realization, with his surrealistic imagination. It was because of his discovery of the old man's body that Unistaire was killed, anyway, not because of his nonsensical remark about Professor MacComerou no longer getting milk—which may at first have been ordered for the old man. Or his listing of all those things out of which he would make a surrealistic picture of the murderer, which had happened to include a wig and a pair of glass eyes. Though that must have jolted Adam Dexter. . . .

Even that last note on the memorandum pad should have told me how long ago it must have been since old Adam sat here and made those notes, in his spidery old hand: "bacon, strawberries . . ." Strawberries in August!

And all that mush out in the kitchen sink!

Coming back here—to resume his role as Professor Adam MacComerou, while he practiced the old man's handwriting, perhaps, and tried to get the old man's money out of the lawyers' hands, at long distance—he had had the problem of supplies, of course. That was why he had ordered all that food in Danbury, enough for a month. He had even used the girl's own ration coupons.

All those provisions that had been on the back porch, as I entered with him from the garden! And on the way back out, after he had alibied himself as Dexter, going back to my stalled car, I had even grabbed a banana from a box, without wondering where that food had come from, with my splitting headache.

He hadn't got old MacComerou's spidery handwriting

yet. That was why he had refused to sign for the special registered letter from the lawyers, of course, when Quelch had
tendered it. That thing had worried me.

How I must have paralyzed him when I appeared, and
said I had come from up the road, and had seen nothing!
I hadn't seen John Flail's body, which he had left there to
show that he had gone on past. He hadn't known that John
Flail had crawled into the ditch.

But it wasn't John, of course. Adam Dexter came rushing
along the road, with Corkscrew dead beside him. He was
going to drop the hat beyond his place, to prove Corkscrew
had gone by. Then he saw John Flail, or one whom he took to
be John Flail, walking along the road ahead of him, probably
returning from working around his place, as he had made
arrangements with John Flail to do. So he had sent his car
hurtling into him. Even better than a hat, John Flail's dead
body would prove that Corkscrew had gone by, and that
Corkscrew was murderous.

And John Flail might have said something—sometime,
to someone—about the old, old man who had been at the
house at first, and who had then disappeared. John Flail was
taciturn and incurious. Still, he had a tongue.

But John Flail was down at his shack. I had seen him
walking away down Swamp Road an hour before. It was
Two-fingered Pete Flail, his brother, whom Dexter struck
and killed, and whom we found in the ditch. Perhaps that
was the moment when Dexter first realized his mistake. He

warned me not to touch the body—he didn't want me to see those missing fingers.

Into his mind there had leaped at once the plan. Here was a body that could be St. Erme's except for the hand—and St. Erme's body, he was realizing, would have to be found. He couldn't use John's own, for John was old and leathery and wrinkled, and his face too well known. After I had left him, and he had found the police were on their way already to inquire about Pete Flail, he had got his car out of the barn, and rushed down to John Flail's.

Had found him eating supper, perhaps, and smashed his head in with a stone. Brought his body back; put it where Pete's had been; and dressed Pete's in his own clothes, with those things done to his face which would both alter Pete's look and enmesh me in it. And removing the hand, of course, with the two fingers. I hope the hand is found.

He had meant to create the illusion that he had gone on up the road, and out at Stony Falls, to have his car found a few days later. He thought he had created the illusion perfectly. After killing Flail and dropping Corkscrew's hat, he had backed on down the road to his drive, and turned up it. Had driven out the station wagon with the flat tire, given his Cadillac in, closed the doors, and driven the station wagon up in front of the doors. In a few days he would drive it somewhere to be found, but in the meantime he didn't want the sun or rain to get on it. He loved that car.

If he had driven just a little farther—just a little farther, after killing Flail—he would have seen that his way was blocked.

Then I came, when he was digging in his garden. I had been stalled on the road an hour, I said. And he realized then that murderous Corkscrew and dead St. Erme and his big gray car, which was nicely reposing in the barn, could not have gone on out to Stony Falls. So they must have turned off down the Swamp Road before they got to me—it was the only way. But I had been right at the Swamp Road, and they couldn't have gone that way, either.

He couldn't get the car on out to Stony Falls, and prove I was crazy or a liar. But he could get it down onto the Swamp Road, and hope to make it stick.

Before my eyes, all the time. If I had only seen. The old man's own huge brown buckram-bound *Psychopathology*, with its dedication to "My Sister Eva," that I had remembered. Wasn't one of the most harrowing cases that he had told of in that book the case of "E. D.," a woman with a homicidal mania whom he had known intimately? Eva MacComerou Dexter, that might have been. I wish I had time to look it up. And to read all those twelve hundred and eighty-seven pages.

Or there is the bright green *Garden Flowers, Their Planting and Cultivation*. That thudding of the spade in the garden that I had heard, as I came up the drive! I might have looked up to see whether tulips are planted in August, and just how they are planted.

Or read *Who's Who in America,* the current edition. Dexter may have torn the page out. But he couldn't think of everything.

Here it is:

MacComerou, Adam Dwight, psychologist. Born Olion, Missouri, June 7, 1862. Educated . . .

1862! I had thought that Dexter looked no more than forty-five, though he could be sixty-five if he said so. But he couldn't have passed with me for eighty-five. Not with those muscles rippling beneath his pale hide.

How could he have had that pale hide, anyway, if he had been working all summer in his garden?

There is this newspaper alone on the desk before my eyes, the newspaper with its big headlines. The evening Danbury paper. Quelch said that the Danbury papers didn't come in by mail till the morning. Stone and Rosenblatt didn't bring it. I hadn't brought it. There had been nothing in Elinor's hands, not even a purse, when I had met her. Yet here was this paper on the desk, fresh from Danbury. It should have told me at once that St. Erme, as I had heard his name, had been in this house—the man who had been in the little ice-cream and stationery store with her in Danbury, and had tossed down his three cents and picked the paper up, and tossed it into the car in front, as they went out and into the grocery.

No one else but St. Erme could have brought that paper here. No one else has come from Danbury.

Everything—everything should have told me.

I'll write his name here:

A. M. DEXTER WAS THE MURDERER. HE IS INIS ST. ERME AND HAS ALSO TAKEN ON THE ROLE OF HIS LATE UNCLE, ADAM MAC-COMEROU, WHOSE BODY LIES IN THE SAW-DUST. DON'T LET HIM GET AWAY WITH IT. RIDDLE.

I'll put it here, beneath the blotter.

There was some paper underneath already, with some writing on it in a spidery hand:

My nephew Adam M. Dexter is coming behind me now to kill me.

A. MacComerou.

He knew. He knew, with all that he knew of murder. But he couldn't help himself.

So he sat here, and wrote that, and slipped it beneath the blotter to be found. But no one ever found it.

Now—

I must not let him hurt her—he's behind me—I see him in the secretary glass, pretending not to look—bat ears, mushy mouth, he has knife, thank God he is going for me first, not girl—name underneath blotter, please find—Dexter—Adam Dexter—killed all—

He had been in the dark bedroom for a long time, I think. He had been in there—he must have been—when I had gone in, looking for Trooper Stone, after waiting twenty minutes. He must have been in there then already, because I closed the window then and locked it, before I came out again.

Behind the curtain in the draped-off corner where clothes were hung, I think, or perhaps just behind the door as I went in. I had smelt him. Yes, I had smelt him. Turning this way and that, to let no shadow get behind me. But I couldn't go in behind the drape and push the hangers full of heavy clothes apart, searching for him, with his knife. I couldn't even look behind the door.

Why he hadn't come at me then I don't know. Except that he must have been wanting me to come in to him. And I was on my toes, I had stance. I kept clear space about me. And so he had thought he had better wait. And I had closed the window and locked it, and gone out and closed the door.

I had figured on the door hinges creaking, if he was in there and came out. But he was a mechanic, and he had an oil can in the bedroom. The hinges had not squeaked.

I felt the shadow on my page, and from the edges of my

eyes I saw him in the glass of the secretary bookshelf, with his pale eyes, his brown bat ears, and mushy mouth.

I didn't want him to do it in here. If the girl waked, with the start of a scream, he would silence her with one slice of that sharp serrated blade.

And I knew that he would rather not do it in here, himself, either, with blood upon the desk and carpet. He would rather do it outside, in the garden, among the yellow roses, with the deep black garden earth in which to hide me, with Corkscrew, so that I should be just vanished.

And so he wanted it, and I wanted it, to be outside in the darkness. On that we were agreed.

I laid down my pencil, yawned, and stretched my arms a little. I had to be very careful. He knew every gesture that I made by nature. He had been watching me all night, trying to read from the least expression or gesture the thought back in my head.

I put my hand back and rubbed the back of my head, and down across the nape. I thought of being hungry. I pushed back my chair and got up, letting the chair leg on my knees roll off onto the carpet. I went out through the kitchen door beside the desk, pausing on the threshold just an instant, to look about me, in front of me, out in the kitchen, as if to make sure that he was not there. I went to the screen door, and removed the pots and pans that were balanced on the chair against the screen, laying them carefully to the side upon the floor. I moved the chair aside, and pulled the screen door open. I stepped out on the latticed porch and got me a banana from the box. I stepped to the porch steps' edge, peeling it.

"Here I am!" he whispered. "Behind you!"

And laughed mushily. Remembering when I had come on him in the garden, maybe, as he had been pounding down the earth above poor old Corkscrew, and the sound of my voice had terrified him, my voice like poor old Corkscrew's, so that he hadn't known whether he had heard it or had only imagined it. Or whether it had come from the twilight air around him, or from the ground. And I had had to use those same words to him, to tell him where I was.

I turned slowly and incredulously, pausing in peeling the banana. As if I could not believe him. Could not believe my own ears. And I felt easier, just a little easier, as I turned slowly to face him. It is better to get it in the breast than in the back. Though about the throat, I don't know.

Don't move, Riddle. Face it.

"You meant to nail me," he said mushily. "You knew from the beginning, from the moment when you came! You knew when you saw the frightened phoebe in the twilight at the drive entrance, because she would not have been frightened if anyone lived here and she was used to seeing men. It was the damned bird that told you!"

"I'm not an ornithologist," I said.

"You knew!" he said. "You knew from the beginning, and you meant to nail me! You knew when you saw that damned wailing cat of Uncle Adam's, that there had been no one to feed, and that hasn't been able to stalk its own game with the bell around its throat. You knew when the damned cat went wailing from you. It was the damned cat that told you!"

"I'm not a zoologist," I said.

"You knew!" he said. "You came to nail me! I read it in your eyes. You knew that I'd not be planting tulip bulbs in August, and pounding them down with a spade. It was that that told you!"

"I'm not a botanist," I said.

"You with your damned quiet soft voice!" he said mushily. "Like that damned red-eyed little bum spouting his Latin. You knew why you had frightened me in the garden! You knew that only St. Erme, besides her, had ever heard his voice, or could recognize it, and so I must be he! Saying to me, 'I am behind you!' When I thought you were in the ground. Hell will not pay for that moment that you gave me. You knew. You knew from the beginning. It was I myself who told you, a dozen times when your damned prodding drove me to. It was I myself who told you. Don't lie to me!"

"Perhaps," I said. "Perhaps I knew from the beginning. Yes, you told me. Everything about you told me. A dozen times, and still a dozen times. Yes, I knew that I had nailed you. My blind throw had hit you. You could slide down beneath grass and lie quietly, but you couldn't get away. You had got it in the head, and you were a dead snake. Yes, I knew, Adam. I knew."

"But you won't ever tell anybody!" he said. "I have been too smart, and I am too strong for you."

He had the knife against my throat. He backed me down the steps, with my arms spread out wide on each side of me from the shoulders, as he wanted them—in his sight, but not overhead, where I might have whipped them down and caught that knife. Step by step backward, down the steps. With the smell of yellow roses and the deep black earth of the garden in the night around me, I stepped back down onto the ground. The ground from which we all come, and to which we all go back someday.

But not for me tonight. I like to think it was the banana peel that finished him—the banana peel that I had thrown away as I went out with him at twilight, starting back up toward my car.

Or perhaps it wasn't. Perhaps I would have got him, anyway. I had nailed him at the Swamp Road, when he had stood behind me with that rock. There had been three times more, at least, tonight, when he had had the chance to give it to me, but there had been fear in him, and he had failed. He knew that I had nailed him. He knew that he was through. So doubtless I should have got him, anyway. But if it hadn't been for that banana peel beneath my right shoe's crepe sole, as I made my third step back upon the ground, before him, I might have been badly cut by that knife.

I felt the sliding peel beneath my foot as I backed, and I smeared my foot with a twist in it, shooting my foot up and throwing my arms back. I caught him in the groin as I went back.

I caught the ground with both hands back of me, and rolled on one hand, half getting my feet beneath me, three feet from his slashing knife. I might have got away from the knife. But he had me on the ground, or half on it, he thought, where he wanted me. He thrust his knife into the waistband of his trousers, quick. He picked up his spade— his spade that he had tossed there, close beside the porch, as we went in at dusk.

The spade had a longer sweep, a more battering stroke, with which to catch me and to smash me. That was his mistake. He sliced the edge of it down at me. It caught me across the instep of my right foot with a smashing blow as I leaped back; and so I had to stand.

The thing was very painful. I shall be lame for a long time. If he had not picked up the spade, I should have got away from him, perhaps. It was what I had counted on doing—my one chance. Dodging the knife thrust and outrunning him, through the tangled rose briers of the garden, and up across the stony pasture in the back, getting him away from the house and the girl in it as Corkscrew had got him away from her down at Dead Bridegroom's Pond, and shouting as I ran. As poor Corkscrew had not had anyone to shout to.

But he had broken the bones of my foot, and I could not get away from him. I was caught there. He had made me stand. He had pinned me with that hellish blow, and I could not move a step from him. And that was his mistake.

The thing was very painful. Yes, extremely. I had no breath to groan about it. I had none at all to shout. I caught the spade shaft as he lifted it to swing it at me again. I got my other hand on it as he tried to slice it down. We gripped it with both our hands upon it, breast to breast.

It was for life. My life, or his, and all that he had counted on. Let him but smash me, and there was no one else who knew him. No one in this world. Not the girl, if she should see him, or hear his mushy voice without his teeth. He could appear again, and say that I had reported falsely that he had been with Unistaire and me down in the sawdust heaps, and that Unistaire had found a dead man there. There would be no need to search the cascaded sawdust heaps further. Let him but bury me beside dead Corkscrew, and I and Corkscrew were one man. Within one hidden grave. Within the black earth at the roots of the yellow roses, vanished. It was my life, or his.

He had strong hands, but I have strong hands, too, as a surgeon must. He had strong shoulders, he had heavy and terribly strong shoulders, muscled like ropes, with a strength that could lift a motor out of its hood housing, or lift up a car by its rear end. But I am supple and wiry, though lightly built. He outweighed me, he outtowered me, by five inches and fifty pounds, but I had twenty-seven years to his forty-five, and I had more years to live for, and better years. We wrestled for that spade.

We wrestled for it, and he was very strong. I shall always remember the knotted sweat of him, and the clenching of his toothless jaws together, and his terrible pale eyes. The sweat and the breath of him, and the ironness of his muscles and his bones. My eyes swam, and the pain of my smashed foot was a red fire. Oh, he was strong, he was very strong. But I was younger than he was by eighteen years, and I knew how his muscles and his bones were made. Slowly I bent him aside, breaking his hold, taking it from him.

He released his grip, as he felt it breaking, and snatched out his saw-tooth knife from his waistband again, with a gasp. He thrust the knife at me, with a quick whipping motion, while from his mouth there came a scream. But I had the spade lifted above his head, and it was coming. I did it with the spade.

Yes, I did it, and I finished it. Right there. My foot was hurting, and I slammed that spade. I felt sick and dizzy. The third blow was unnecessary, I grant it; but I was sick and dizzy. My foot will always hurt whenever I smell black garden earth or yellow roses, so long as I live, I think.

Lieutenant Rosenblatt has given me a cigar. A Havana Corona, soft and green, as I am particularly fond of them. I don't allow myself to smoke frequently, since a surgeon must keep his nerves and eyes at the keenest, and his mind always on the sharpest edge. Still, as Rosenblatt said in presenting it, it is something of an occasion.

And I think so, too. To be given a cigar by a policeman. I know something else that I'd rather be given, by that sweet youngster Darrie still sleeping in the living room. But that can wait.

"*Da mi mille basia, diende centum,*" said old Catullus, in

his next line following that melancholy one about us humans having one long night for sleeping, after our suns go down. I have no confidence in my Latin any more, and I'll have to ask her to translate it for me. "Give me a thousand kisses, then a hundred"—I think that's the way it should be. But we shall see.

Rosenblatt has a brother who is a police sergeant in Tampa, is why he has such good green cigars, he says. Orange blossoms and cigars are the loveliest products of Florida.

Rosenblatt has given Stone a cigar, too. I had to take care of Stone before I could take care of my own foot. A rather nasty mess back of Stone's right ear, at the posterior junction of the parietal and temporal, just forward of the lambdoidal suture. Enough to kill any two ordinary men. But before we had got him in through the window, from the deep grass outside where he was lying, and onto a bed, Stone was awake and swearing. There are some bone splinters that will have to be taken out, and he'll probably need a plate, but he is actually smoking that cigar. Rosenblatt thinks it is funny that Stone was knocked out by a stone. Two stones and one bird, he says. A buzzard. But everyone has his own sense of humor.

That buzzard got Stone by scratching his fingernail on the window screen beside Stone's head and showing his face. Stone had been asleep, and didn't know that Unistaire had found Professor MacComerou dead and buried in the sawdust heaps, and that men were digging for his body. This was Professor MacComerou at the window, and he lived here.

He had been helping to direct the search. He had been help-ing all night.

Dexter whispered through the screen to Stone that Lieu-tenant Rosenblatt wanted Stone to go down to Unistaire's house and phone the Hotel President from there to check up on St. Erme, particularly to see if they could get any finger-prints of St. Erme from the room he had occupied, to com-pare with the fingerprints of that mutilated body, without letting Miss Darrie know. And to Stone, still half asleep— or even wide awake, as he claims he was—that seemed an intelligent order. He had unhooked the screen and taken it out quietly, and had slid quietly forth to join Professor Mac-Comerou.

Dexter had got him just as his toes reached the ground, with his hands behind him on the window ledge, as I had figured it. A blinding flash is all that Stone remembers.

Dexter had run like hell, after getting him, back up to the woods behind the house, and up along the path which led to John Flail's, letting out that awful scream from there which had pulled Rosenblatt raging forth: "This is Quelch! Help! Help! I've got him!" He had waited till Rosenblatt had passed him, and had then returned, slipping in through the screenless window into the bedroom, and had waited there for his chance when I should not be watching.

Rosenblatt hadn't believed in the least that that scream came from Quelch, of course, he says. Even if Quelch had been dying, he had felt quite sure that Quelch would not refer to himself as anything but Mr. Quelch. He had known it was the killer—Corkscrew or St. Erme, or whoever it was, not having made up his mind between the two of them— and he was mad enough to try to find out. He hadn't figured that the call was to lure him away from the house, but that it was directed toward the men down in the swamp, with the dogs, to lure them back from there. And so he had stayed out looking, feeling sure that Stone had come out of the bedroom immediately to take over the guard on the girl, or else I would have shouted to him to return before he had got out of earshot.

It was his fault, he says, for taking Stone for granted. But it was my fault, too.

So it was a rock that he had used to get Stone, and the spade that he had used to try to finish me. He had used the car to kill Two-finger Pete Flail, and a rock, as with Stone, to crush in the head of John Flail. And he had strangled poor old Corkscrew with his hands. He had used the knife on Corkscrew only after he was dead, to have some blood on the car and the road. Actually, he had used the knife only once to kill—on Unistaire in the sawdust pits, when there had been no other weapon handy, and Unistaire had to be silenced at once about the body he had found.

But the fear of that knife had been plenty.

"Taking it all in all," Rosenblatt has just remarked, "it was a pretty good play, as criminal plays go. He had established himself as Professor MacComerou from the time of his first arrival with his uncle, and his alibi that he had been living here continuously for the past ten or twelve weeks was plausible, except for what John Flail could have told. No one would have thought of looking in the barn here for that car. It had passed here and killed John Flail. And so, by an assumable sequence of actions, it had gone on and on. He had got Miss Darrie's money, and even though he had failed to kill her, all that could be said about St. Erme, when she should eventually discover her emptied bank account, was that he must have been a crook. But that was no blight on himself as Dexter, who didn't know St. Erme very well. He might very likely have got St. Erme's insurance eventually, even without a body. Still, he must have felt that Pete Flail's body was rather providential. It's always better when you're dead to have a body."

"It's better when you're alive, too," I told him. "There were some moments when I wasn't sure that I hadn't traveled out of mine, without knowing it, I'll admit now, Lieutenant. But I just had to stand on it that I had been there at the Swamp Road entrance all the time, and that he had not gone by. I'm sorry if I drove you wild with keeping at it."

Rosenblatt grinned. "I believed you," he said. "In a way. I had a feeling that you had nailed something, I mean. But I couldn't see just what. It was too simple and obvious, I suppose. Like the card you had in your pocket, which named him all the time."

"What card?" I said.

He handed me a pasteboard.

"I was looking through your jacket, that you had left on the front seat of that coupe of yours, while you were down at the sawmill," he said apologetically. "You had this card in your side pocket. The killer's name and address, and all."

I took it from him. It was the card which had been given to me by old John Buchanan's housekeeper, with the address of the dealer to whom I was to deliver the car, and which I had thrust away in my pocket, together with the envelope containing the fee, without looking at it. I looked at it now.

Dexter's Day & Nite Garage
614 West 14th Street, N. Y. C.
Tel.: Mordaunt 2-8350

Cars Bought and Sold, Top Prices

A. M. Dexter,
Professor of Automobilistics,
Proprietor.

And on it the housekeeper had written four words, with an arrow pointing to the name: "This is the man."

In my pocket all the time.

I thought again, as I put the card away without a word, of that instructor from Harvard whom I had had at Southern State, who had always objected with such outraged horror to being addressed as professor. A professor, he had said, was a high-school manual-training teacher, a piano player in a honkytonk, or the proprietor of a flea circus. Old Adam MacComerou of *Homicidal Psychopathology*, with all his degrees and all that was in his brain, had never called himself professor on his mailbox or in big red *Who's Who in America* or on the title page of his book itself, when I thought of it. Maybe he would rather be struck dead than be called professor.

Well, he had been. No one had ever called him professor or doctor to his face, anyway—old A. MacComerou with his great old brain that had known so much of murder. Yet that bald-skulled naked marble-eyed goon had introduced himself to me as "Professor MacComerou" in the garden in the twilight when I had first come upon him, and I had swallowed it. He had been a professor, all right. A professor of automobilistics. And I had asked him for a garage man.

I nodded toward the living-room door, as Rosenblatt got up to leave the bedroom and find a phone.

"What do you have to tell her when she wakes up?" I said.

"What is there to tell?" he said.

"Nothing but that it was all a nightmare," I said. "A bad dream without reality."

"That's all it ever was," he said.

And that is all it will ever be between her and me. A man came into her life and vanished. A spade dropped on my foot and hurt it. Though I shall limp a little when I smell yellow roses and black rich garden earth, all through life.

THE END

DISCUSSION QUESTIONS

- Were you able to predict any part of the solution to the case?

- Aside from the solution, did anything about the book surprise you? If so, what?

- Did any aspects of the plot date the story? If so, which ones?

- Would the story be different if it were set in the present day? If so, how?

- What role did the setting play in the narrative?

- If you were one of the main characters, would you have acted differently at any point in the story?

- Did you identify with any of the characters? If so, who?

- Did this novel remind you of anything else you've read? If so, what?

- Did anything strike you about the form of the narrative?

AMERICAN MYSTERY CLASSICS

from

PENZLER PUBLISHERS

*Available now
in hardcover and paperback:*

Charlotte Armstrong . . . . *The Chocolate Cobweb*

Charlotte Armstrong . . . . *The Unsuspected*

Anthony Boucher. . . . . *Rocket to the Morgue*

John Dickson Carr . . . . *The Crooked Hinge*

John Dickson Carr . . . . *The Mad Hatter Mystery*

Mignon G. Eberhart. . . . . *Murder by an Aristocrat*

Erle Stanley Gardner . . . . *The Case of the Careless Kitten*

Erle Stanley Gardner . . . . *The Case of the Baited Hook*

Frances Noyes Hart . . . . *The Bellamy Trial*

H.F. Heard. . . . . *A Taste for Honey*

Dorothy B. Hughes . . . . *Dread Journey*

Dorothy B. Hughes . . . . *The So Blue Marble*

Frances & Richard Lockridge . . . . *Death on the Aisle*

John P. Marquand . . . . *Your Turn, Mr. Moto*

Stuart Palmer . . . . *The Puzzle of the Happy Hooligan*

AMERICAN MYSTERY CLASSICS

from

Charlotte Armstrong
The Unsuspected

Introduction by Otto Penzler

To catch a murderous theater impresario, a young woman takes a deadly new role . . .

The note discovered beside Rosaleen Wright's hanged body is full of reasons justifying her suicide—but it lacks her trademark vitality and wit, and, most importantly, her signature. So the note alone is far from enough to convince her best friend Jane that Rosaleen was her own murderer, even if the police quickly accept the possibility as fact. Instead, Jane suspects Rosaleen's boss, Luther Grandison. To the world at large, he's a powerful and charismatic figure, directing for stage and screen, but Rosaleen's letters to Jane described a duplicitous, greedy man who would no doubt kill to protect his secrets. Jane and her friend Francis set out to infiltrate Grandy's world and collect evidence, employing manipulation, impersonation, and even gaslighting to break into his inner circle. But will they recognize what dangers lie therein before it's too late?

CHARLOTTE ARMSTRONG (1905-1969) was an American author of mystery short stories and novels. Having started her writing career as a poet and dramatist, she wrote a few novels before *The Unsuspected*, which was her first to achieve outstanding success, going on to be adapted for film by Michael Curtiz.

"Psychologically rich, intricately plotted and full of dark surprises, Charlotte Armstrong's suspense tales feel as vivid and fresh today as a half century ago."
—Megan Abbott

Paperback, $15.95 / ISBN 978-1-61316-123-4
Hardcover, $25.95 / ISBN 978-1-61316-122-7

Anthony Boucher
Rocket to the Morgue

Introduction by F. Paul Wilson

A Golden Age mystery set in the world of science fiction in its early days

Legendary science fiction author Fowler Faulkes may be dead, but his creation, the iconic Dr. Derringer, lives on in popular culture. Or at least, the character would live on, if not for Faulkes's protective and greedy heir Hilary, who, during his time as the inflexible guardian of the estate, has created countless enemies in the relatively small community of writers of the genre. Fully aware of his unpopularity, Hilary fears for his life after two near misses with potentially mortal "accidents" and calls the police for help. Detective Terry Marshall and his assistant, the inquisitive nun, Sister Ursula, will have to work overtime to keep him safe—a task that requires a deep dive into the strange, idiosyncratic world of science fiction in its early days.

ANTHONY BOUCHER (1911-1968) was an American author, editor, and critic, perhaps best known today as the namesake of the annual Bouchercon convention, an international meeting of mystery writers, fans, critics, and publishers. Born William Anthony Parker White, he wrote under various pseudonyms and published fiction in a number of genres outside of mystery, including fantasy and science fiction.

"Stellar."—*Publishers Weekly* (Starred Review)

Paperback, $15.95 / ISBN 978-1-61316-136-4
Hardcover, $25.95 / ISBN 978-1-61316-135-7

John Dickson Carr
The Crooked Hinge

Introduction by Charles Todd

An inheritance hangs in the balance in a case of
stolen identities, imposters, and murder

Banished from the idyllic English countryside he once called home, Sir John Farnleigh, black sheep of the wealthy Farnleigh clan, nearly perished in the sinking of the Titanic. Though he survived the catastrophe, his ties with his family did not, and he never returned to England until now, nearly 25 years later, when he comes to claim his inheritance. But another "Sir John" soon follows, an unexpected man who insists he has absolute proof of his identity and of his claim to the estate. Before the case can be settled, however, one of the two men is murdered, and Dr. Gideon Fell finds himself facing one of the most challenging cases of his career. He'll soon confront a series of bizarre and chilling phenomena, diving deep into the realm of the occult to solve a seemingly impossible crime.

JOHN DICKSON CARR (1906-1977) was one of the greatest writers of the American Golden Age mystery, and the only American author to be included in England's legendary Detection Club during his lifetime. Under his own name and various pseudonyms, he wrote more than seventy novels and numerous short stories, and is best known today for his locked-room mysteries.

> "An all-time classic by an author scrupulous
> about playing fair with his readers"
> —*Publishers Weekly* (Starred Review)

Paperback, $15.95 / ISBN 978-1-61316-130-2
Hardcover, $25.95 / ISBN 978-1-61316-129-6

Erle Stanley Gardner
The Case of the
Careless Kitten

Introduction by Otto Penzler

*Perry Mason seeks the link between a poisoned kitten,
a murdered man, and a mysterious voice from the past*

Helen Kendal's woes begin when she receives a phone call from her vanished uncle Franklin, long presumed dead, who urges her to make contact with criminal defense attorney Perry Mason; soon after, she finds
herself the main suspect in the murder of an unfamiliar man. Her kitten has just survived a poisoning attempt, as has her aunt Matilda, the
woman who always maintained that Franklin was alive in spite of his
disappearance. It's clear that all the occurrences are connected, and that
their connection will prove her innocence, but the links in the case are
too obscure to be recognized even by the attorney's brilliantly deductive
mind. To solve the puzzle, he'll need the help of his secretary Della Street,
his private eye Paul Drake, and the unlikely but invaluable aid of a careless but very clever kitten.

ERLE STANLEY GARDNER (1889-1970) was the best-selling American author of the 20th century, mainly due to the enormous success of his Perry Mason series, which numbered more than 80 novels and inspired a
half-dozen motion pictures, radio programs, and a long-running television
series that starred Raymond Burr.

> ### "One of the best of the Perry Mason tales."
> ### —New York Times

Paperback, $15.95 / ISBN 978-1-61316-116-6
Hardcover, $25.95 / ISBN 978-1-61316-115-9

OTTO PENZLER PRESENTS
=AMERICAN MYSTERY CLASSICS=

Frances Noyes Hart
The Bellamy Trial

Introduction by
Hank Phillippi Ryan

A murder trial scandalizes the upper echelons of Long Island society, and the reader is on the jury...

The trial of Stephen Bellamy and Susan Ives, accused of murdering Bellamy's wife Madeleine, lasts eight days. That's eight days of witnesses (some reliable, some not), eight days of examination and cross-examination, and eight days of sensational courtroom theatrics lively enough to rouse the judge into frenzied calls for order. Ex-fiancés, houseworkers, and assorted family members are brought to the stand—a cross-section of this wealthy Long Island town—and each one only adds to the mystery of the case in all its sordid detail. A trial that seems straightforward at its outset grows increasingly confounding as it proceeds, and surprises abound; by the time the closing arguments are made, however, the reader, like the jury, is provided with all the evidence needed to pass judgement on the two defendants. Still, only the most astute among them will not be shocked by the verdict announced at the end.

FRANCES NOYES HART (1890-1943) was an American writer whose stories were published in *Scribner's*, *The Saturday Evening Post*, where *The Bellamy Trial* was first serialized, and *The Ladies' Home Journal*.

"An enthralling story."—*New York Times*

Paperback, $15.95 / ISBN 978-1-61316-144-9
Hardcover, $25.95 / ISBN 978-1-61316-143-2

Dorothy B. Hughes
Dread Journey

Introduction by
Sarah Weinman

A movie star fears for her life on a train journey from Los Angeles to New York...

Hollywood big-shot Vivien Spender has waited ages to produce the work that will be his masterpiece: a film adaptation of Thomas Mann's The Magic Mountain. He's spent years grooming young starlets for the lead role, only to discard each one when a newer, fresher face enters his view. Afterwards, these rejected women all immediately fall from grace; excised from the world of pictures, they end up in rehab, or jail, or worse. But Kitten Agnew, the most recent to encounter this impending doom, won't be gotten rid of so easily—her contract simply doesn't allow for it. Accompanied by Mr. Spender on a train journey from Los Angeles to Chicago, she begins to fear that the producer might be considering a deadly alternative. Either way, it's clear that something is going to happen before they reach their destination, and as the train barrels through America's heartland, the tension accelerates towards an inescapable finale.

DOROTHY B. HUGHES (1904–1993) was a mystery author and literary critic famous for her taut thrillers, many of which were made into films. While best known for the noir classic *In a Lonely Place*, Hughes' writing successfully spanned a range of styles including espionage and domestic suspense.

"The perfect in-flight read. The only thing that's dated is the long-distance train."—*Kirkus*

Paperback, $15.95 / ISBN 978-1-61316-146-3
Hardcover, $25.95 / ISBN 978-1-61316-145-6

Frances and Richard Lockridge
Death on the Aisle

Introduction by Otto Penzler

They say Broadway is a graveyard of hopes and aspirations, but someone's adding corpses to its tombs...

Mr. and Mrs. North live as quiet a life as a couple can amidst the bustle of New York City; Jerry, a publisher, and Pamela, a homemaker, the only threat to their domestic equilibrium comes in the form of Mrs. North's relentless efforts as an amateur sleuth, which repeatedly find the duo investigating murders and sundry other crimes. So when the wealthy backer of a play is found dead in the seats of the West 45th Street Theatre, the Norths aren't far behind, led by Pam's customary flair for murders that turn eccentric and, yes, humorous. Alongside Lieutenant William Weigand of the New York Police Department, they'll employ illogical logic and bizarrely tangential suggestions to draw the curtains on a killer.

Frances and Richard Lockridge were two of the most popular names in mystery during the forties and fifties. Inspired by Richard's series of non-mystery stories for *The New Yorker* about a publisher and his wife, Mr. and Mrs. North, the Lockridge husband-and-wife duo collaborated successfully to write twenty-six mystery novels about the couple, which, in turn, became the subject of a Broadway play, a movie (starring Gracie Allen), and series for both radio and television.

"Delicious ... an enormously engaging old-school mystery"
—*Booklist* (Starred review)

Paperback, $15.95 / ISBN 978-1-61316-118-0
Hardcover, $25.95 / ISBN 978-1-61316-117-3

John P. Marquand
Your Turn, Mr. Moto

Introduction by
Lawrence Block

An American pilot of dwindling fame slips from grace in Tokyo, and lands in the hands of Japan's most cunning spy...

During World War I, Casey Lee was one of the best pilots around. But now the war's over, the Depression is on, and Lee is washed up and desperate for work. When a tobacco company suggests he fly from Japan to North America, a feat which has never been accomplished, Lee jumps at the opportunity, but the idea is abandoned soon after he arrives in Tokyo. Stranded in a foreign land with wavering loyalty to his home country, Lee has few friends, but his situation changes suddenly when he meets the intriguing Mr. Moto, a Japanese man who takes a particular interest in the down-and-out pilot. By the time he meets Sonya, Moto's beautiful Russian colleague, Casey has unknowingly entered into a life-threatening plot of international espionage at the service of Japan's imperial interests — but will he realize the severity of his situation before it's too late?

JOHN P. MARQUAND (1893–1960) was a Pulitzer Prize–winning author, best known for his satirical novels lampooning New England high society. Marquand was also a regular contributor to the *Saturday Evening Post*, where, in the serialized *Your Turn, Mr. Moto* (originally titled *No Hero*) he debuted the wildly successful Moto character.

"A gifted storyteller"—*Washington Post*

Paperback, $15.95 / ISBN 978-1-61316-157-9
Hardcover, $25.95 / ISBN 978-1-61316-156-2

Stuart Palmer
The Puzzle of the Happy Hooligan

Introduction by Otto Penzler

After a screenwriter is murdered on a film set, a street-smart school teacher searches for the killer.

Hildegarde Withers is just your average school teacher—with above-average skills in the art of deduction. The New Yorker often finds herself investigating crimes led only by her own meddlesome curiosity, though her friends on the NYPD don't mind when she solves their cases for them. After plans for a grand tour of Europe are interrupted by Germany's invasion of Poland, Miss Withers heads to sunny Los Angeles instead, where her vacation finds her working as a technical advisor on the set of a film adaptation of the Lizzie Borden story. The producer has plans for an epic retelling of the historical killer's patricidal spree—plans which are derailed when a screenwriter turns up dead. While the local authorities quickly deem his death accidental, Withers suspects otherwise and calls up a detective back home for advice. The two soon team up to catch a wily killer.

STUART PALMER (1905–1968) was an American author of mysteries, most famous for his beloved Hildegarde Withers character. A master of intricate plotting, Palmer found success writing for Hollywood, where several of his books were adapted for the screen.

"Will keep you laughing and guessing from the first page to the last."—*New York Times*

Paperback, $15.95 / ISBN 978-1-61316-104-3
Hardcover, $25.95 / ISBN 978-1-61316-114-2

Ellery Queen
The Siamese Twin Mystery

Introduction by Otto Penzler

Ellery Queen takes refuge from a wildfire at a remote mountain house — and arrives just before the owner is murdered...

When Ellery Queen and his father encounter a raging forest fire during a mountain drive, the only direction to go is up a winding dirt road that leads to an isolated hillside manor, inhabited by a secretive surgeon and his diverse cast of guests. Trapped by the fire, the Queens settle into the uneasy atmosphere of their surroundings. Then, the following morning, the doctor is discovered dead, apparently shot down while playing solitaire the night before.

The only clue is a torn six of spades. The suspects include a society beauty, a suspicious valet, and a pair of conjoined twins. When another murder follows, the killer inside the house becomes as threatening as the mortal flames outside its walls. Can Queen solve this whodunnit before the fire devours its subjects?

ELLERY QUEEN was a pen name created and shared by two cousins, Frederic Dannay (1905-1982) and Manfred B. Lee (1905-1971), as well as the name of their most famous detective.

> "Queen at his best ... a classic of brilliant deduction under extreme circumstances."
> —*Publishers Weekly* (Starred Review)

Paperback, $15.95 / ISBN 978-1-61316-155-5
Hardcover, $25.95 / ISBN 978-1-61316-154-8

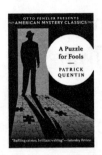

Patrick Quentin
A Puzzle for Fools

Introduction by Otto Penzler

A wave of murders rocks an asylum—and it's up to the patients to stop them

Broadway producer Peter Duluth sought solace in a bottle after his wife's death; now, two years later and desperate to dry out, he enters a sanitarium, hoping to break his dependence on drink—but the institution doesn't quite offer the rest and relaxation he expected. Strange, malevolent occurrences plague the hospital; and among other inexplicable events, Peter hears his own voice with an ominous warning: "There will be murder." It soon becomes clear that a homicidal maniac is on the loose, and, with a staff every bit as erratic as its idiosyncratic patients, it seems everyone is a suspect—even Duluth's new romantic interest, Iris Pattison. Charged by the baffled head of the ward with solving the crimes, it's up to Peter to clear her name before the killer strikes again.

PATRICK QUENTIN is one of the pseudonyms of Hugh Callingham Wheeler (1912-1987), who collaborated with several other authors on the books written as by Q. Patrick and Jonathan Stagge. Wheeler was born in London but moved to the United States in 1934 and became a U.S. citizen, as did one of his writing partners, Richard Wilson Webb; he also collaborated with Martha (Patsy) Mott Kelly.

> "Another absolute gem unearthed by Otto Penzler and included in his American Mystery Classics series....What a find!"
> —*Booklist* (Starred Review)

Paperback, $15.95 / ISBN 978-1-61316-125-8
Hardcover, $25.95 / ISBN 978-1-61316-124-1

Clayton Rawson
Death from a Top Hat

Introduction by Otto Penzler

A detective steeped in the art of magic solves the mystifying murder of two occultists.

Now retired from the tour circuit on which he made his name, master magician The Great Merlini spends his days running a magic shop in New York's Times Square and his nights moonlighting as a consultant for the NYPD. The cops call him when faced with crimes so impossible that they can only be comprehended by a magician's mind.

In the most recent case, two occultists are discovered dead in locked rooms, one spread out on a pentagram, both appearing to have been murdered under similar circumstances. The list of suspects includes an escape artist, a professional medium, and a ventriloquist, so it's clear that the crimes took place in a realm that Merlini knows well. But in the end it will take his logical skills, and not his magical ones, to apprehend the killer.

CLAYTON RAWSON (1906–1971) was a novelist, editor, and magician. He is best known for creating the Great Merlini, an illusionist and amateur sleuth introduced in *Death from a Top Hat* (1938).

"One of the all-time greatest impossible murder mysteries."
—*Publishers Weekly* (Starred Review)

Paperback, $15.95 / ISBN 978-1-61316-101-2
Hardcover, $25.95 / ISBN 978-1-61316-109-8

Craig Rice
Home Sweet Homicide
Introduction by Otto Penzler

The children of a mystery writer play amateur sleuths and matchmakers

Unoccupied and unsupervised while mother is working, the children of widowed crime writer Marion Carstairs find diversion wherever they can. So when the kids hear gunshots at the house next door, they jump at the chance to launch their own amateur investigation—and after all, why shouldn't they? They know everything the cops do about crime scenes, having read about them in mother's novels. They know what her literary detectives would do in such a situation, how they would interpret the clues and handle witnesses. Plus, if the children solve the puzzle before the cops, it will do wonders for the sales of mother's novels. But this crime scene isn't a game at all; the murder is real and, when its details prove more twisted than anything in mother's fiction, they'll eventually have to enlist Marion's help to sort out the clues. Or is that just part of their plan to hook her up with the lead detective on the case?

CRAIG RICE (1908–1957), born Georgiana Ann Randolph Craig, was an American author of mystery novels, short stories, and screenplays. Rice's writing style was unique in its ability to mix gritty, hard-boiled writing with the entertainment of a screwball comedy.

"A genuine midcentury classic."—*Booklist*

Paperback, $15.95 / ISBN 978-1-61316-103-6
Hardcover, $25.95 / ISBN 978-1-61316-112-8

Mary Roberts Rinehart
Miss Pinkerton

Introduction by Carolyn Hart

After a suspicious death at a mansion, a brave nurse joins the household to see behind closed doors

Miss Adams is a nurse, not a detective—at least, not technically speaking. But while working as a nurse, one does have the opportunity to see things police can't see and an observant set of eyes can be quite an asset when crimes happen behind closed doors. Sometimes Detective Inspector Patton rings Miss Adams when he needs an agent on the inside. And when he does, he calls her "Miss Pinkerton" after the famous detective agency.

Everyone involved seems to agree that mild-mannered Herbert Wynne wasn't the type to commit suicide but, after he is found shot dead, with the only other possible killer being his ailing, bedridden aunt, no other explanation makes sense. Now the elderly woman is left without a caretaker and Patton sees the perfect opportunity to employ Miss Pinkerton's abilities. But when she arrives at the isolated country mansion to ply her trade, she soon finds more intrigue than anyone outside could have imagined and—when she realizes a killer is on the loose—more terror as well.

MARY ROBERTS RINEHART (1876-1958) was the most beloved and best-selling mystery writer in America in the first half of the twentieth century.

"An entertaining puzzle mystery that stands the test of time."—*Publishers Weekly*

Paperback, $15.95 / ISBN 978-1-61316-269-9

Hardcover, $25.95 / ISBN 978-1-61316-138-8

Mary Roberts Rinehart
The Haunted Lady

Introduction by Otto Penzler

Someone's trying to kill the head of the Fairbanks estate, and only her nurse can protect her.

The arsenic in her sugar bowl was wealthy widow Eliza Fairbanks' first clue that somebody wanted her dead. The nightly plagues of bats, birds, and rats unleashed in her bedroom were the second indication, an obvious attempt to scare the life out of the delicate dowager. So instead of calling the exterminator, Eliza calls the cops, who send Hilda Adams—"Miss Pinkerton" to the folks at the bureau—to go undercover and investigate.

Hilda Adams is a nurse, not a detective—at least, not technically speaking. But then, nurses do have the opportunity to see things that the police can't, and to witness the inner workings of a household when the authorities aren't around. From the moment Adams arrives at the Fairbanks mansion, confronted by a swarm of shady and oddball relatives, many of whom seem desperate for their inheritance, it's clear that something unseemly is at work in the estate. But not even she is prepared for the web of intrigue that awaits her therein.

Mary Roberts Rinehart (1876-1958) was the most beloved and best-selling mystery writer in America in the first half of the twentieth century.

"Twisty and atmospheric ... a worthy addition to the American Mystery Classics series."
—*Publishers Weekly*

Paperback, $15.95 / ISBN 978-1-61316-160-9

Hardcover, $25.95 / ISBN 978-1-61316-159-3

Cornell Woolrich
Waltz into Darkness

Introduction by
Wallace Stroby

*From "the supreme master of suspense" comes the
chilling chronicle of one man's descent
into madness. (New York Times)*

When New Orleans coffee merchant Louis Durand first meets his bride-to-be after a months-long courtship by mail, he's shocked that she doesn't match the photographs sent with her correspondence. But Durand has told his own fibs, concealing from her the details of his wealth, and so he mostly feels fortunate to find her so much more beautiful than expected. Soon after they marry, however, he becomes increasingly convinced that the woman in his life is not the same woman with whom he exchanged letters, a fact that becomes unavoidable when she suddenly disappears with his fortune.

Alone, desperate, and inexplicably love-sick, Louis quickly descends into madness, obsessed with finding Julia and bringing her to justice—and simply with seeing her again. He engages the services of a private detective to do so, embarking on a search that spans the southeast of the country. When he finally tracks her down, the nightmare truly begins…

CORNELL WOOLRICH (1903–1968) was one of America's best crime fiction writers. Famous for suspenseful and dark plots, his work inspired more films noir than that of any other author.

"A richly embroidered tapestry … this is classic noir well worthy of a revival"—*Booklist*

Paperback, $15.95 / ISBN 978-1-61316-152-4

Hardcover, $25.95 / ISBN 978-1-61316-151-7